Cross Road Blues

Galactic Blues Book 1

by

D.L. Martone

Copyright © 2021

D.L. Martone

All rights reserved.

For Andy and Chris,

two brothers who have given us unwavering support

Note: *Cross Road Blues: Galactic Blues Book 1* was originally published in late 2018 as four weekly serials—*Born Under a Bad Sign, Call It Stormy Monday, Mean Old World*, and *That's All Right*. The text has since been reedited and expanded to fit its current form.

For more information, visit the authors' website:
dlmartone.com

Chapter
1
REMY

The bridge of the *R.L. Johnson* shook. Captain Remy Bechet bolted awake in his chair. This wasn't the ship's resigned kind of shudder, reminding him of her general age and dislike of gravity fields. Nope, this was a *we've-got-company* kind of shake.

Blades.

His eyes darted around the room, automatically seeking Dreyla. There she was, unharmed, poring over the nav console, seeming as cool as ever. A customary mass of black curls concealed her face as her slim, athletic frame leaned against her station, a tight grip on it the only sign of tension.

She could've woken him sooner, dammit. Before getting attacked by what appeared to be three blades.

Make that four... Crap. Five.

The silver ships swooped into the vision of the *R.L. Johnson*'s front windows, in a mocking V formation. He'd expected this, of course. No one could steal a large shipment of TZ107 chips and assume there would be no heat. Valuable as the power source for many things in the solar system, the Teez also served as hard currency out here in the Belt, an impoverished market where money was hard to come by, legally or otherwise. The shipment of Teez they'd stolen was worth half a billion credits, a huge score, and not one to go unnoticed. Or unpunished.

Only one thing for it. They'd have to take the ship deeper into the Belt.

Remy's gaze locked onto his adopted daughter's. Dreyla was doing a good job of not looking petrified.

"Port side took a hit, Captain," she reported. "Second-degree damage to the airlock, and one of the boosters is out."

He nodded, relaxing his grip on the old-fashioned steering wheel he'd reclaimed from a 1968 Corvette, and shifted his primary focus from the main viewscreen to the adjacent gun-turret display. He'd designed this setup himself so he could operate the steering wheel with his left hand and the joystick controlling the forward guns with his right.

It was one of the many modifications he'd initially made to the ship after buying her. Though he'd enabled each station, from navigation to diagnostics, to control almost all the ship's systems, steering was the only action with a single point of access, naturally from his station.

As with the rest of his well-worn ship, the bridge had seen better days. True, it was spacious, with a main steering console that curved along the front bulkheads, plus two smaller consoles behind him, one on each side of the bridge. All the buttons and displays functioned effectively, at least most of the time, but a noticeable patina had spread across every surface, from the walls to the consoles themselves.

The *R.L. Johnson* was old but true, and with any luck, she'd save their asses again, as she had countless times before.

Remy scanned the central viewscreen, noting the five blades currently cramping his style. Though he'd always enjoyed piloting his own ship, he knew it was time to engage the A.I. system. For the moment, he needed to focus on blasting those blades to hell while the ship's computer took over steering.

The *R.L. Johnson* (or *Jay*, for short) had sustained numerous hits over the years, and she was still flying, but he didn't want to test the limits of abuse she could tolerate. He slammed one of the guns into operation and rubbed some dirt off the targeting visor with his thumb.

One fine day, I'll clean this baby up.

"Find me a route through the Holcom Range," he growled at Dreyla. "And where the hell is Sache?" His second gunner should be here.

Dreyla frowned, her bottom lip protruding, a groove deepening between her dark eyes. "The *Jay*'s way bigger than those blades. They'll have an easier time flying through there than we will."

He grinned. "Honey, nobody has an easy time flying through there... but nobody flies the Belt like I do."

Chapter 2

LILLY

Sheriff Lilly Greyson swatted a stubborn sandfly from her vision. As if the burning sun weren't enough, she had to deal with these annoying insects, too. Intent on eating out her eyeballs, they were driving her slowly insane and generally making her day worse. What quirk of terraforming had permitted them to flourish?

Well, she wouldn't let anything, terraformed or organic, stop her from busting those asswipes today.

Behind her, Deputies Davis and Brand were swatting

their own paths clear, waiting for her call to action. She eavesdropped on their hushed conversation. Davis, a tall, fit young man, swarthy and handsome, had been trying to flirt with newbie Brand, a trim, blonde, twentysomething beauty, all week.

Guess now he has his chance.

"Know what the Rot is, right?" Davis asked.

"Respiratory disease caused from breathing in Vox7," Brand responded. A textbook answer.

Clearly, no one close to her had been affected. Not surprising, given her status as a recent immigrant to the planet.

"Shortness of breath at first," Davis clarified, "then the painful breathing, and eventually... bleeding lungs. It's called the Rot because it feels like you're rotting from the inside out."

Lilly swatted another fly away from her nose and shook her dark ponytail to discourage any of its pals. If this was Davis's best attempt at flirting with Brand, then there'd be no action between her two deputies anytime soon.

And that's fine with me.

"But it's treatable?" Brand asked in a too-girlish voice.

"Well, only one way to live any kind of normal life after you get it... you gotta shoot up with nano-biotics every ninety days," her colleague explained. "Miners need the meds to stay alive, but anyone living on Vox relies on regular injections to keep the Rot away."

Lilly turned, gesturing to the abandoned warehouse they were approaching, the sort of place where black-market deals notoriously went down. "And these bastards are selling fake nano-biotics, Deputy Brand... selling them to greenhorn miners fresh off the ship, letting them believe they'll be safe." She continued forward. "We should force them to work in one of the community mines, catch the Rot, and deal with it without the meds." Grinning, she glanced over her shoulder. "My jail is way too good for them."

Brand's pretty eyes widened. Davis opened his mouth, as if to say something, but Lilly held up her hand for silence. A few more paces, and they'd be within hearing distance of the warehouse. The time for chatter was over.

The domed, cream-colored building had been one of the first structures hastily erected after the discovery of Vox7. Nearly sixty years old now—and looked every day of it. Lilly strode ahead, up the five steps to the front entrance. Pursing her chapped lips together, she pushed her shoulder against the door. To her surprise, it swung open easily under the pressure. Good sign or bad? She couldn't tell, but to be safe, she indicated her deputies should keep close behind her.

The gloomy interior offered a respite from the sun and the flies, but the stale odors of dust, urine, desiccated rodents, and assorted debris urged Lilly to take shallow breaths. When a moment passed, and no welcoming party appeared, she relaxed a little, but kept her hand pressed against her holster, ready to draw her pistol if necessary. While they might have tracked down a bunch of scumbags here, she knew that other people, from trouble-seeking teenagers to some of Naillik's homeless population, often used the building. She didn't want to shoot anyone that didn't deserve it.

Lilly and her two deputies moved down the main corridor, their standard-issue boots making little noise. Though the warehouse might have been state-of-the-art when first assembled, its features and furnishings were long out of date. Wall-mounted monitors were cracked and broken. Layers of dust coated the walls and other surfaces, just like everywhere else in and around Naillik. Some of the inner walls had even crumbled, as they weren't meant to last more than a few years. Typical terraforming mentality, resulting in a typical ghost building.

But farther along the lengthy corridor, obvious signs of life emerged: Certain hallways were well worn and free of dust. Somebody or something was regularly cleaning the floor.

A small thud compelled Lilly to draw her pistol and swing it up toward an open room to her right. A scruffy man and an even more unkempt woman froze in fear as they eyed the weapon pointing at them. Lilly glanced down at the bed beside their dusty shoes. Actually, it resembled more of a nest, as if they'd piled up various pieces of foam insulation, probably from the compromised inner walls, into a makeshift sleeping space.

Lilly couldn't tell if these were some homeless, down-on-their-luck miners or if one of them were about to turn a trick. Frankly, she didn't care. Slowly, she lowered her gun and holstered it, then put a finger to her lips to indicate the couple should keep quiet. Neither the man nor the woman nodded in compliance, but when they didn't make a sound either, Lilly and her deputies left them to their business and resumed their search for the vermin uppermost on their minds.

Chapter 3

DREYLA

Dreyla Bechet rolled her eyes at her captain's boast. Her swaggering surrogate father might be one of the most skilled men she knew, but it would be refreshing if he didn't always think he was. Then again, she often found comfort in his total faith that he could haul everyone's asses out of whatever mess they'd gotten into. Because there was no shortage of messes in a pirate's way of life.

Lately, they'd endured so many close calls she'd taken to using adrenaline blockers just to fall asleep. She hadn't told Remy about those yet. For all his scruffy bravado and grease-splotched clothes, he was a clean-veined guy who held an anti-quated notion that music alone (and maybe a good shot of whiskey) could calm the nerves, and he expected the same standards of her. Speaking of which...

The twangy strains of old blues artist, Robert Leroy Johnson, blasted onto the bridge, almost drowning out the whines of torpedoes ripping the *Jay*'s energy shields to shreds. Dreyla didn't care what Remy had said about the so-called American legend. Every creaking strum of his acoustic slide guitar and every soulful note of his pleading voice jangled her nerves.

She wished the captain wouldn't play anything at all. When enemy guns were tearing their ship to pieces, communication was challenging enough without having to deal with the noise Remy considered *classic*. He could at least blare something better than the old-man tunes he preferred. She'd once tried convincing him to play one of her favorite modern pop groups instead, but that had gone about as well as expected. He'd kept it on for roughly five seconds before declaring it junk and going back to the oldies.

Predictably, the tune now resounding from the ship's speakers was "Cross Road Blues," one of Remy's favorite in-a-tight-space, under-serious-attack songs. Naturally, he had a different track for every occasion.

"What did I say about playing that music?" she asked.

"That it was badass and inspiring?"

"Yeah. The precise term was *don't*." She rubbed her temples, shifted her attention to the nav console, and frowned at the screens displaying the hell outside.

The five United Nations Space Force ships were smaller than the *Jay*, but not ineffectual. Called blades because of their sleek, deadly look, the UNSF ships resembled massive sushi knives hurtling through space with the intent of hacking up the enemy at will.

Dreyla's official job as navigator—official now that she'd turned sixteen, despite the fact that she'd been doing it for four years—was to determine safe routes through asteroid belts and any other hazardous places, while Remy flew the ship (unless, of course, he was distracted by warfare). So, as much as she longed to help him fight off the enemy, she needed to focus on her own job and trust he could handle his alone.

Just then, the door whooshed open, and Newman Sache entered the bridge at a trot. "Sorry," the second gunner said, wincing. "Taking a leak."

"Yeah. Glad you could join us." Remy cocked his head at the starboard window. "Take those. I'm on these."

The sounds of an explosion cut through Dreyla's concentration. Where once a blade had been slicing a path way too close to the *Jay*'s port side (the captain's current focus), there now appeared a billowing cloud of metallic debris, dispersing in the blackness of space.

"Pretty," she remarked, rewarding Remy with a tiny smile.

"See, you just need the right music for the job. Save your fusion hip-hop for when we're cleaning the cargo hold."

"We never clean the—"

Another massive explosion drowned out her words. She yelped as the aftershock rattled through her, crunching her bones together inside her stiffened limbs. This time, the *Jay* had taken a direct hit, and she couldn't immediately tell from which side.

"Holy crap," Remy yelled.

A bead of sweat trickled from his dark, silver-streaked hairline, down his clenched jaw, and into the collar of his shirt as he pumped the blaster for all it was worth, all the while yelling commands in staccato at poor Newman. Judging by the ferocity of the swearing, her captain wasn't as on top of the situation as he'd initially claimed.

She tapped the edges of her console, wishing she could help her crewmates shove some of those blades into the next dimension. Or at least tackle something more energetic than just waiting here. But she had her task. The computer had almost figured out the route. The tracing algorithm, if left on its own, would do a brute-force search through all the possibilities, taking hours they didn't have. By chopping it up, though, with some quick and dirty optimization heuristics she had a particular knack for, she could speed up the operation.

It was enough. It had to be. While waiting for the computer to finish, she found herself drumming her fingers in time to the music, which annoyed her. She stopped before Remy noticed.

"Hah!" Newman shook out his blond curls. He'd hit a UNSF ship, too, sending the disabled hulk careening off course. He winked at her. "Captain's not the only one with good aim around here."

Dreyla gave him a curt nod. "Yeah, just three more to go, Flash."

A ping from her console sounded.

Bingo.

The algorithm had coughed up the route. Working fast, she locked it into Remy's station so he could access the details and, when able to concentrate on steering again, fly the ship accordingly. For now, she'd have to rely on the A.I. system to handle the task.

Meanwhile, by unspoken agreement, she'd stay on the nav controls to fine-tune the route on their suicide trek. If they were going to die, she didn't want it to result from her error.

As the two men kept blasting, and the vessel shuddered under response attacks, Dreyla closed her mind to everything except nudging the ship in different directions, reining the *Jay* back on course whenever a jolt threw her off. She felt at one with the route planner and with her fellow bridge members. Usually, their cooperation worked like a well-oiled machine, one they'd utilized many times, to slip out of many tight spaces. With any luck, that would be the case yet again.

Dreyla and the two men whooped in unison when one of the blades crashed into a small asteroid they'd only narrowly avoided themselves. Its crew was probably using automatic navigation, prone to miscalculations in this weird quantum asteroid belt that didn't seem to follow the standard laws of physics.

A little burst of hope ignited in the pit of her stomach. Maybe, just maybe, they'd get out of this mess alive, even with those fifty thousand, high-value Teez chips in the cargo hold. Maybe Remy's massive gamble had paid off.

The spark of hope flared into full-blown elation when the darkness of the screen told her they'd lost their remaining two pursuers, who must've fallen behind in the maze of asteroids in the *Jay*'s wake. She turned to Remy, letting the blissful silence speak for itself. Grinning smugly as usual, he spread his hands in an *I-told-you-so* fashion. She felt a wave of magnanimity for him and, yes, even his crappy music.

"Time to play your victory song?" she asked.

Remy wiped his brow. "I like your thinking, Drey, but we're not out of the woods yet."

Chapter 4

LILLY

Lilly continued her methodical trek down the corridor, her two deputies trailing her closely. She could sense their nerves were on edge. Davis would be alright. Brand, on the other hand, was probably too green to have joined this kind of op.

But beggars can't always be choosers.

Based on the lights here and there, Lilly knew the building still had power, which meant the solar panels mounted on the roof were still functioning. Despite that, many of the light fixtures were broken, so she found it tough to see inside some of the windowless areas of the warehouse. In fact, the pattern of darkened spots seemed deliberate, compelling Lilly to head for the darkest hallway off the main artery. Luckily, the emergency lights on her and her deputies' tactical jackets emitted enough of a reddish glow to avoid stumbling into the debris strewn across the path.

At the far end of the corridor, a band of amber light stretched from beneath a closed door. When a shadow drifted across the beam, Lilly stopped and held up a hand to halt her deputies. In the tense silence, she heard rapid, shallow breaths coming from Brand. She wanted to send her back to the transport vehicle, but it was too late now.

"Wait for my signal," she whispered to Davis, who nodded in return.

She drew her gun, nudged the door open a fraction, and tried to assess the situation. Illuminated by an overhead light and at least one curtain-free window, the room resembled a former medic station. Through the crack in the door, she could see two bare cots against one wall and an array of defunct monitoring equipment.

Lilly carefully widened the gap. Seated behind an out-of-place desk was the familiar shape of Yercer Taul, a broad, meaty man with a menacing goatee, steely eyes, and a bald head that glowed under the lighting. An open crate, presumably containing the fake nano-biotics, sat atop the desk.

Lounging by one of two dust-coated windows were three of his lackeys, all skinnier and shorter than their boss, dressed in casual, unassuming garb but armed with powerful guns. Nearest to Lilly stood two down-on-their-luck miners who seemed barely better off than the pair of vagrants she'd just seen in the makeshift bedroom. Worse, they appeared to be negotiating with Yercer.

"Three hundred credits," he said in a deep, matter-of-fact tone. "You won't get better value in town or anywhere out along the Rim."

Lilly doubted that. Even if the nano-biotics he was selling weren't counterfeit, the miners could probably find a better deal elsewhere. Especially where desperation flourished, like in the mining areas along the canyon rim that partially encircled the town of Naillik.

She took a slow, steady breath. Three hundred credits amounted to more than a month's salary for a miner.

Bastard.

Yercer was one of Gono Darkbur's top lieutenants, quite skilled in extracting money from those who could least afford it. A few trusted informants had told her that he might be trying to set up shop in Naillik.

Yeah. Over my dead body.

18

After nodding at her deputies, Lilly swung the door open, held up her repulsor pistol, and pointed it at Yercer. Davis and Brand flanked her on either side, just as they'd been trained to do in such a situation.

"Drop your weapons," Lilly ordered, not taking her eyes off Yercer.

The man's eyes lit with amusement. "Ah, the lady sheriff, stepping into her old man's shoes... now that he's dead and buried. Pretty little thing that you are. How touching."

"How 'bout I touch you with this?" Lilly inched nearer, aiming her pistol at Yercer's barrel chest.

Though the energy wave wouldn't kill him, it could knock him out long enough to cuff him and drag him back to her station for questioning. Plus, it would hurt like hell.

In a surprisingly swift move, Yercer leapt to his feet, propelled his chair sideways, and darted toward the two hapless miners. Using them as a partial barrier, he grabbed them both by the scruff and retreated toward a rear exit. Barely out of their teens, the two guys probably regretted ever stepping foot on the arid planet.

Grunting with disgust, Lilly followed Yercer and his reluctant human shields across the room. Given his height, he couldn't fully hide behind the two miners, so she took her chance and aimed at his smirking face. Unfortunately, one of her shots whizzed by Yercer's shoulder, while another hit one of the poor miners in the chest. The luckless young man staggered and fell, and without a second glance, Yercer left him sprawled on the ground as he continued to drag the second miner toward the exit.

Behind her, Davis and Brand fired off rounds, keeping Yercer's three lackeys at bay. Lilly paused to ensure they had the situation under control, hoping she'd be free to concentrate on snagging Yercer. Just as she turned, though, she spied one of Brand's wayward shots hit the already weakened perimeter. Large cracks resembling lightning forks spread across the plaster, and a second later, a huge chunk of wall collapsed with a mighty groan, bringing part of the ceiling down on her deputies and two of Yercer's lackeys.

The room filled with acrid dust. Lilly coughed and her eyes watered, but she didn't have the luxury of checking on her deputies under the rubble. Yercer had pulled out a gun with his free hand, and even worse, the last minion standing had joined him and was now aiming his weapon at her, too.

She fired at the skinny guy, sending him flying back against another wall, where he slumped to the ground. Ducking instinctively, she avoided the blast that Yercer shot off. Then she responded in kind, hitting him right in the center of his chest.

Nice.

Except... instead of dropping, Yercer just twitched, as if swatting away a fly. He was an enormous, muscular guy. And seriously tough. But still, the blast should have had more of an impact.

"Lady, you insult me," Yercer mocked. "Coming at me with such a paltry weapon."

He smirked at his lackey still wincing in pain, which gave Lilly just enough time to reach into her other hip holster and pull out her big blaster. She enjoyed seeing Yercer's widening eyes through the viewpoint of her ultra-deadly KV-360 weapon. Maybe she should have started with this one—and forgone questioning entirely.

The bastard'll only lie anyway.

"How is this for an insult?" she taunted.

"Now hang on a moment, Sheriff." For the first time, Yercer's voice revealed a smidgeon of doubt.

Just like all the other scum and useless bureaucrats she'd had to deal with during her initial year as Naillik's sheriff, he couldn't show the slightest bit of respect until his freaking life depended on it.

"That's more like it," she growled, stepping around him and prodding the tip of her gun into a wad of muscle flanking his spine. "Now, let's try this again. Drop your weapon."

Reluctantly, he tossed it on the floor, just as his

wounded lackey wobbled to his feet and the other two minions crawled from beneath the rubble.

"You're all useless," Yercer grumbled.

Lilly pressed her gun against his beefy back. "Tell your lackeys to fall in line, and we'll make this nice and civilized-like."

Yercer nodded sullenly at his minions. The trio meekly dropped their weapons and clustered beside him while Davis and Brand emerged from the rubble, dirty as all hell but apparently unscathed.

With his friend's help, the miner she'd inadvertently stunned also rose to his feet. Together, the two would-be buyers scurried into the darkened corridor. Lilly allowed herself a sigh of relief, grateful she hadn't permanently harmed an innocent.

"Move," she barked at Yercer, indicating he should lead the way outside, through the rear exit.

Compliant but clearly pissed, he opened the door, stepped into the blinding sunshine, and ventured around the exterior of the warehouse. Lilly occasionally prodded him forward, as her deputies did the same with the three lackeys behind her, but she didn't relax until they'd cuffed and packed the four criminals into the back of their transport vehicle, along with the crate of fake nano-biotics.

Arresting Yercer was a terrific score for her and her people, but life back at the sheriff's station would surely get interesting now. And not in a good way.

Chapter 5

REMY

Despite some damage from the trigger-happy UNSF blades, the *Jay* had made it through the swirling mass of asteroids and certain death, otherwise known as the Holcom Range. They'd beaten the odds once again. It was becoming a habit.

Remy released the joystick and swung back to his main controls. "Piece of cake," he said to Newman.

No response.

"Newman?"

His second-in-command looked ready to pass out, his face paler than the icy surface of Europa. Same shell-shocked expression his gunner wore after every engagement.

"It's OK, Newman. We did good."

Newman gazed at him, wide-eyed. "Don't know how much longer my nerves can take flyin' with you, Cap." He shook his head a couple times, blinked his eyes, and inhaled deeply.

Remy glanced at Dreyla.

She raised her eyebrows, then gave him a quick smile. "I'm getting the route up for our rendezvous with Tyson on Bernhal 3," she said.

"Good. Thanks, Drey."

His buoyant mood deflated at this reminder of the next stage of their mission. Tyson Milstone, powerful, corrupt, and dog-ugly, was the director of mining who had provided Remy with the blueprints for the Yertie Commons mining facility—Tyson's direct competition. How the hell he'd managed to get his hairy hands on that information, Remy didn't know. And didn't really care.

All that mattered was that the info had allowed him and his crew to bust into the Yert, as the miners called it, grab the goods, and get the hell out again. That was the extent of what he'd needed to know.

"Tyson should pay us more," Newman grumbled. "After all that UNSF business."

"Yeah, we coulda done without that little plot twist," Remy agreed. "But if you think we're gonna get a fraction more than what Tyson agreed to with Larker Max, then that asteroid field has clearly rattled your brain."

Newman grunted and smoothed back his hair, which seemed a little grayer than it had before the firefight. "Maybe I'm getting too old for this pirating business."

Remy laughed. "Old? You ain't old. *Tosh* is old." To be fair, he didn't know the exact age of the ship's doctor. Legend suggested a hundred and fifty, but that couldn't be right. "Why, you're just a wee babe in Tosh years."

"That old man's only got himself to blame," Newman muttered. "Should have the good sense to know when to pass on."

Dreyla, who was munching on a protein bar, hurled the balled-up wrapper at him.

"What?" Newman grinned, finally starting to relax again.

"Tosh is the best doc in the Belt," she replied, "and he's..."

"Stoned all the time," finished Newman.

"So?" She shrugged. "He's a sweetie."

Chuckling, Remy tapped a spot beneath his console, and a concealed compartment popped open, revealing his antique, but still deadly, .45 Colt. Relishing the stress-free moment, he leaned back in his chair and polished the piece with the hem of his shirt.

"Captain, main power's going offline," Dreyla informed him.

Remy nodded, lowered the pistol to his lap, and sank against the headrest. Was it time for him to go offline, too, and grab the overdue sleep that had eluded him for two days? Maybe some whiskey would dull the adrenaline spiking in his system.

After ensuring that Dreyla was looking elsewhere, he opened another hidden compartment beneath his console. Just as his fingers closed around the neck of a bottle of Jack Daniels, the comms unit crackled.

"Cap, something's goin' on," Tosh's creaky voice uttered through the speaker.

Speak of the devil.

But the old man didn't sound right. There was an edge to his words that made Remy's hair stand on end. He released the whiskey bottle, slammed the compartment door shut, and turned off the blues.

"Can you be more specific?"

"I found Brinx dead."

Remy's stomach plummeted to his boots and shot back up again to punch him in the solar plexus. Brinx was the strongest guy on the ship and sharp as a blade. "What? How?"

"Multiple stab wounds. And his throat was cut."

Remy grabbed his Colt and leapt from his chair. His two crew members on the bridge were staring at him. They'd heard

Tosh, too.

"Drey, stay on nav," he ordered. "Newman, I think we have a mutiny on our hands."

"I hate mutinies," Newman grumbled.

"Yeah, I'm not a fan either." Remy slapped on the emergency controls at his station.

"You'll blow a hole in the ship with that cannon," Dreyla said, nodding at the Colt.

"Hey," Remy replied, shooting her a manic grin. "It's me."

Apparently, she wasn't buying his tough-guy act. "I should go with you."

"Nope. You're staying right here, safe on the bridge."

Remy turned to Newman, who stood beside his console, his lips pursed, a plasma pistol gripped in his hand.

"Come on, Grumpy," Remy said. "Let's get this over with."

He cocked his head and led the way off the bridge, aiming for the medbay and wishing the break between crises had lasted a little longer.

Chapter 6

LILLY

Lilly kept the transport vehicle running at top speed by overriding its auto-control. The more time Yercer Taul spent outside the reinforced cell with his name on it, the more she endangered Brand, Davis, and herself, not to mention the entire community of Naillik.

Nobody had spoken since they'd driven off. As she jerked the steering wheel from side to side, Lilly kept replaying the moment the ceiling had come crashing down. They had gotten lucky. If Brand's gun had penetrated the support beams, the whole damn thing could have collapsed. She and her deputies would all be dead, and worse, Yercer might be roaming free, peddling his fake meds to unsuspecting miners.

The two deputies squashed beside her stared steadfastly ahead. Davis alternately fiddled with his holster and gripped the overhead handle for support. Brand, at the side window, winced as each cloud of sand and dust rained against the vehicle, as if she'd never experienced a sandstorm before. Both of them were likely still on edge from what had happened.

As Lilly crested over the next dune, the platinum-alloy roof of her sheriff's office gleamed in the distance. The enormous building had been dropped out of orbit, in sections, courtesy of the Vox Council. When the original building had been destroyed in an attempt to take out Naillik's law enforcement a year ago, she had wanted the new one built on-planet, by people she knew and trusted. In the end, the Council and the home world had decided otherwise, choosing to send the pieces from the other side of the galaxy. Typical bureaucratic crapola. The top floor hadn't even arrived until two months ago.

She swung into the parking lot beside the office and turned to her deputies. "Taul and his boys are thirsty and in mean moods, so when I say be careful, what I mean is... any crap from them and you shoot 'em where it hurts without hesitation." She'd mainly directed this at Brand, who of the two would be the most likely, due to inexperience, to screw up the delicate operation of transferring scum from vehicle to cell.

"Got it, boss," Brand chirped in her precise voice. "Where it hurts."

30

Davis shot her an incredulous look before pulling his sunglasses down over his eyes.

Lilly stepped out of the vehicle and waited until her deputies had done the same before pressing the control pad to open the back doors. The four criminals blinked at the sudden daylight. They were handcuffed to each other, packed in so tightly that even without restraints they wouldn't have been able to move much. She should have brought the larger transport vehicle, but she hadn't expected to arrest four people.

Eh, good enough for them.

"Alright, folks," she hollered before Yercer could open his mouth and take control of the conversation. "Right this way. Make it snappy and we can all get out of the heat."

After a moment's hesitation, they clambered out of the vehicle, Yercer giving Lilly the stink eye before jerking his meaty head around to take in the surroundings. He then leered down at Brand who, to Lilly's dismay, shrank under his gaze.

Davis swiftly produced his gun and prodded Yercer and his men forward with such force that Lilly didn't have to intervene. While she was sure Davis wanted to bed Brand, he was still professional enough to pick up the slack and deal with the situation before it had gotten out of hand. Assisting the newer deputies was a required part of the job. With the high turnover in staff, either due to death or simply because being a deputy didn't pay that well, Lilly needed the newbies trained fast, and she depended on the veterans to step up when needed.

The streets of Naillik were crowded in the midday rush. Hovercraft and wheeled transports jostled for space down the main street. Pedestrians scuttled between vehicles and building entrances under the protection of sun-brellas—the ultra UV-resistant umbrellas that could double as weapons when necessary.

For a town of only twenty-six thousand citizens, it shouldn't be this crowded, but the actual number was five times higher if you considered all the mining establishments and camps within Naillik's territory. The population along the Rim was something conveniently left out of the discussion when Tim had initially accepted the job of sheriff ten years ago. Not that it would have changed his mind any.

Back then, in happier times, just after they'd gotten married, Tim had been fired up over his new job. His sense of right and wrong had come directly from his upbringing, since both of his parents had served in the military. He'd wanted to create a haven in this backwater corner of the galaxy that even families could inhabit.

After his death, Lilly had honored his ambition by taking up the role of sheriff. Sure, she had trouble envisioning this place as ever being family-friendly, but that didn't make the bad guys good. She just wanted to tip the balance on the side of justice and give as many bastards as possible what they deserved before she relinquished the job.

A couple with two kids shuffled along the sidewalk, slow enough to catch her attention. At least two of them, the mother and son, had the Rot. Dried blood streaked their faces below their nostrils. Hell, the father and daughter probably had it as well.

Roars from across the street yanked her attention away. The ruckus was coming from inside a small bar, the Lost Last, which most patrons called the Double L—a lot easier to say when you were drunk. The doors burst open and a small crowd rumbled onto the street, hollering and cheering.

"Another fight?" Brand asked.

"Well, it is Tuesday." Lilly rolled her eyes at Brand's nonplussed expression. "There's a fight at the Double L every day."

"Should we stop it?" her newest deputy asked.

"Have at it." Lilly strode toward the prisoners. They were craning their necks, trying to watch the fight with the glee of inmates observing an in-prison riot.

"That's the difference between you pussy Nailliks and those of us who live in Bane," Yercer said, sidling as close to her as his restraints allowed. "We like a good fight."

Lilly jammed her elbow into his ribs, urging him to back off.

"You're right." She grinned. "That did feel good."

He growled at her but didn't attempt anything stupid.

The crowd had grown to almost a hundred as passersby stopped to watch. This was a bad look for Naillik. Lilly didn't want to see her town turn into another Bane—a lawless city in a constant state of chaos. This kind of crap was bad for business, even hers.

She had two jobs, after all. One that kept order and one that benefited from it.

True, she never thought she'd want to own—or even have a partial stake in—a saloon, a brothel, and a hotel. But she couldn't be sheriff forever. And she had to admit, when she and Tim had bought into the Red Lady, it had provided more revenue than being the sheriff did, or ever could.

Luckily, it was a classier joint than the Double L and easily brought in more than ten times its revenue. Now that she was on her own, with a lot of dangerous enemies, she had to look after herself—because no one else sure as hell would.

She glanced at Yercer, who eyed her as if he wanted to crack her skull open.

"Both of you, go stop that fight," Lilly said to her deputies. "I've got these guys."

"Think you can control all of us?" one of Yercer's lackeys piped up.

Lilly held up a remote and, without hesitation, pushed a button to shoot an electrical current through all their restraints. She was egalitarian like that.

They writhed in pain, tugging their wrists in the electrified handcuffs.

"Pretty sure," she replied.

"Stop it," one whimpered.

She removed her finger from the remote button.

Recovering quickly, Yercer stepped toward the idiot who'd spoken and, before Lilly could separate them, headbutted the lackey, hard enough to produce a loud thud. The guy staggered around dizzily, threatening to pull them all down with him. Including his boss.

Lilly grinned, finding it both amusing and predictable whenever a criminal's ego and ire overrode his reason.

"OK, Sheriff," Davis agreed. "We'll take care of the brawl." He strode off, tugging Brand after him.

Lilly, meanwhile, led her four prisoners into the building. The last thing she heard was Brand using her amplified comms unit to yell at the crowd, her precise accent cutting sharply through the air, followed by an unusually awed silence. She shrugged. Maybe her new recruit would get the hang of this after all. That was good. With Yercer intent on sucking all her attention, she would need all the help she could get.

Chapter 7

REMY

The ship was eerily quiet as Remy and Newman rushed through the carbon-alloyed passageways. They could hear little beyond their own footsteps and the humming of the ambience controllers and life support. Without the normal chatter of human voices, the thump of the air coolers sounded like the *Jay*'s heartbeat.

"It has to be either Joss or Abrams," Newman said in a tense whisper behind Remy.

"Reckon you're on to something there," Remy said. "Seeing as they're the only other crew members an' all."

He pressed the control button to open the outer door of the medbay corridor, his gun poised to shoot. This was the most likely place for an ambush.

The inner corridor was empty.

"Course, seeing as they're inseparable," Remy continued in a murmur, "it's most likely both."

It was hard to believe that Redi Abrams, his top-notch mechanic, would've chosen the mutinous path. He was one of the most reliable fixers in the Belt. Of course, Remy had steadily shifted more responsibilities to Dreyla, which he knew Abrams didn't like. But Remy had little choice: She was twice as smart as the much older man.

The reclusive burglar, Urgon Joss, was a different story. While he was tight with Abrams, he'd never really ingratiated himself with the rest of the crew. Damn, though, the man could get into anything... any lock, safe, building, or ship. Was he the type that would kill a fellow crew member? If he were honest with himself, Remy knew the answer.

He and Newman didn't even reach the medbay before Tosh staggered out, his grizzled face and grayish, straw-like hair looking wilder than ever.

Remy grabbed the old man's forearm. "You hurt, Doc?"

"Nearly, but no," Tosh panted. "Joss and Abrams are headed to the cargo hold." With a quavering finger, he needlessly indicated the direction.

"Get back inside," Remy said, nudging him toward the medbay. "No arguing." He turned to his other crewmate. "Come on, Newman."

Dammit!

Of course, the mutineers would've gone to the cargo hold—where the loot was. If he'd been thinking straight, he would've headed there first. Now running through the passageways, he and Newman approached the cargo hold fast, and he had no plan other than to shoot first and ask questions later. If anyone was left to answer them.

Just as he pressed the entrance button, a plasma blast hit the wall, way too close to his left hand. Sparks shot off the metallic surface and whipped across his fingers. Remy jerked his Colt in the direction of the shooter and motioned Newman to slip behind him.

Abrams stood in the middle of the cargo hold, his bald head and muscular shoulders poking out over the large pallet of Teez chips. It took Remy a few moments to adjust to the reality of his mechanic as the enemy. His dark eyes reflected a mean emptiness, as if the two of them were strangers, as if he hadn't worked with Remy these past few years and had his ass saved by the captain on more than one occasion.

So much for gratitude.

"Cover me!" Remy yelled to Newman and dove into the cargo hold.

He slammed against the wall behind a giant stack of smuggling crates as Abrams took repeated shots at him. Remy was grateful the containers were made of the strongest alloy he could afford.

But where was the other mutineer? His gaze darted around the hold. If Joss were here, he wouldn't be sitting idly by. He must be headed to the bridge.

Crap, no. Drey...

Remy wished he'd thought to seal her inside. His only choice now? To get back to the bridge as quickly as possible.

"Come out in the open, Captain. Do this like a man," Abrams said in a voice Remy hardly recognized.

"I'm nice and cozy just where I am," Remy snarled back.

A barrage of shots hit the wall behind him. As with the rest of his ship, the inner walls of the cargo hold had seen better days and weren't exactly blast-proof. Hopefully, the *Jay* would hold up.

Through a slit between crates, he could see Abrams moving back and forth, as if trying to find a good angle.

"You don't have to do this, Abrams," Remy called out. "Look, if this is a comment on my leadership, hell, I get it. I can be an ass sometimes. Why don't I give you a raise?"

Abrams let off another volley of shots, making the crates tremble. "This is a whole lot bigger than you, Capt'n. It ain't personal."

The shots knocked a crate off the top of the pile. The metal-alloy box collided with Remy's arm as it toppled to the floor, sending white-hot pain through his bones. He unleashed a howl. This was starting to feel very personal indeed.

"You ain't got long, Capt'n," came the mechanic's voice, laced with a note of satisfaction. "Sorry it's gotta end like this. See, Larker never wanted you to succeed with the job, and if you did, me and Joss were to make sure you didn't make it back alive, even if the shipment did."

Remy blinked in pain and amazement. He always knew his boss, Larker Max, was the scum of the universe, but this was low even by his standards.

A movement behind him made him twist his gun around to the entrance. Newman hovered by the side of the doorway.

Before Remy could yell at him, Abrams shot at his new target. Newman bent over, clutching his shoulder.

Abrams advanced toward his wounded crewmate, who hadn't yet sought cover. Remy jumped up to block him and pushed over a wall of crates, which tumbled to the floor. There was a loud crash, followed by a muffled yell, as the crates swallowed Abrams up. But judging by a movement within the heap a few seconds later, it hadn't killed him. Unfortunately.

"Allow me," Newman said, clenching his jaw and brushing past Remy to inspect the pile of crates.

"No," Remy shouted, lowering the Colt and reaching out to grasp Newman.

Like a manic jack-in-the-box, Abrams poked out and shot Newman at close range. Remy's gunner also managed to get a shot off, right through the mechanic's forehead, but then he, too, collapsed.

Remy dove forward to catch Newman. Spotting a large, ragged hole in the older man's chest, Remy knew the sad truth: Tosh wouldn't be able to patch him up.

He looked sorrowfully into Newman's pale blue eyes, which gradually grew duller.

Newman whispered something, and then his head lolled, lifeless, to the side. His final words turned Remy's blood cold.

"Hurry. Dreyla."

Chapter 8

DREYLA

Dreyla let loose a string of colorful curses as she stood before the *Jay*'s power display along the rear wall of the bridge. No one was around to hear her anyway. It wouldn't help to bring the main power back online, but it sure did make her feel better.

What the hell?

Even the backup units wouldn't come on, and unfortunately, she couldn't fix any of them from here.

"Abrams disconnected the main power coupling in the engine room," Urgon Joss said, sauntering onto the bridge.

Dreyla turned at the sound of his voice. His thin cheeks

stretched into a macabre grin as he stood with his hands on his hips, watching her.

Her blood froze. The situation was suddenly clear. All the life force seemed to drain from her body, and she had to compel her legs to take deliberate steps toward her nav console. It was her only hope.

"Don't even bother trying to contact the captain." Joss stepped closer. "He's dead by now... the ship is ours."

"You piece of crap," she hissed.

Dead. The captain? No, it's not possible.

She hurled herself at the console, slapping on the comms button with the heel of her hand. "Captain, you need..."

A whack against her jaw made everything turn black. Next thing she knew, she was sprawled on the ground, clutching at the floor plates, aching from the impact. Her eyes watered, but primal instincts of rage guided her now. She jerked her chin up. Joss was charging at her again.

His hands reached under her arms as if to hoist her to her feet. Kicking furiously to hide her intentions, she slid her emergency blade out of its hidden pocket on her hip. Then she stopped moving, twisted, and deftly sliced Joss's forearm. A deep red gash appeared across his flesh.

He roared. His grip on her armpits slackened and she wriggled out. He stared at the cut as if he couldn't believe what she'd done, but then his face clouded over and he shot her a death glare. She braced herself, gripping her blade's handle still tighter behind her back. If she was going to die, at least she'd go down fighting.

With one outstretched arm dripping with blood, Joss lunged at her. This time, she bent low and sank the blade into his thigh, piercing through the thick overalls. He shrieked and howled, grasping the inflicted leg, but he didn't have the guts to pull the blade out. Dreyla straightened up and shuffled backwards, heading toward the comms unit again.

His hand flashed in her periphery before it collided against her skull with such force it toppled her over, making her crash helplessly against the steel-edged panel of the nav console.

Through the mist of pain, she could see he was about to pluck the blade from his thigh. The menacing light in his eyes was more animal than human. She couldn't believe she'd had civil conversations about engine diagnostics and power conversions with this guy earlier in the day—though, admittedly, the thief's mechanical curiosity seemed rather suspicious now.

His eye-watering attempt to remove the knife halted at the sound of footsteps clattering on the corridor to the bridge.

He isn't dead!

Using the diversion, Dreyla clambered to her feet. But

Joss was quicker. He grabbed her shoulder, spun her around, and tugged her back into his chest, just as Remy entered the bridge. Joss's strong fingers dug into her collarbone, and she could smell his awful breath.

She met Remy's eyes for a fraction of a second before he moved his gaze to Joss.

"Abrams is dead," the captain said. "Your little mutiny is over."

She felt the cool tip of Joss's gun pressing against her temple. She tried, for Remy's sake, not to look like she was ready to throw up with fear.

"You don't get it, Bechet," Joss sneered in his nasally voice. "But you're done. Larker set this whole thing up. He wanted you dead."

Remy's eyes narrowed. "Why?"

She knew the captain was using the talking tactic to buy time, or maybe because the info was important. But he didn't know how unhinged Joss had become. She tried to signal him with her eyes, but other than blinking rapidly, she couldn't think how else to convey *shoot now!*

"Too many of the other crews started looking to you," Joss continued. "Larker Max doesn't like competition."

"I never wanted what he has," Remy grunted.

"I told him that, told him you were weak... that you would only kill to protect your people, not to finish a job."

Joss shoved his fist against Dreyla's spine, making it

clear he wanted her to move. She pressed back with all her weight, slowing their path toward the exit. Every second counted.

"That's why I'm gonna walk this little tart to the cargo hold," Joss said with another belligerent shove. "And she and I, and the Teez, are going out through the airlock."

"Why the hell would you do that?" Dreyla spat. She might as well play the info-extraction game, too.

"He's got ships coming in," Remy answered coolly for him. "I'm assuming that if you didn't take the *Jay*, you'd just drop out and be retrieved by one of them."

"So, you ain't as dumb as you look," Joss said.

"That's up for debate." Remy gave him a sardonic smile. "But I can't let you take her."

"Got no choice." Joss stepped closer to the exit, shoving her along. "We both know you won't risk the girl's life, so as long as I got her, you ain't doin' a damn thing."

Dreyla threw Remy a desperate look. Joss was right. Remy wouldn't take the shot while he had her.

She wanted to be all heroic and scream, "Never mind me!" but she really, really didn't want to die. And definitely not like this.

"Who's coming for you?" Remy asked, edging closer to Joss.

"An old friend of yours. Personally, I find her even scarier than Larker." Joss let out a low chuckle of relish.

Dreyla knew exactly which "old friend" Joss meant. The woman who would like nothing more than to unceremoniously blast off Remy's arm—which was, in all fairness, what he'd done to her—and who, once she'd finished shooting off other appendages, would eventually kill him. Possibly by disembowelment.

"So, you're working for that bitch, too," Remy stated rather than asked.

Joss nodded. "She's part of the deal, and it pays a helluva lot more than you do."

"Can't enjoy that money," Remy said slowly, "if you're dead."

The quirk in Remy's tone tipped Dreyla off. Following his gaze, she reached down and grabbed the handle of the blade still sticking out of her captor's thigh and gave it a ruthless twist. He hollered in pain. His vise grip on her loosened so she could duck down below his shoulders.

Remy's gun hand was up in a flash, firing straight at Joss's head. The shot predictably hit the target, and the former burglar lost all grip on her as he sank to the ground.

Dreyla moved so quickly that Remy hardly had time to lower the gun. She collapsed against his chest and hugged her captain... her protector... her father. He enfolded her in a tight squeeze. All the fear transformed into a wave of euphoria at their both being alive. Nothing else mattered.

"Drey... holy crap, Drey," he murmured, his voice

hoarse, sounding lost.

Tosh bounded in, faster than Dreyla had ever seen the old man run. "Anyone need medical attention?"

Remy released her from the embrace, and they all stood back to regard the man sprawled at their boots.

Tosh bent closer to peer at the hole in Joss's head. "Guess not."

"We need to reconnect the power coupling in the engine room," Dreyla said, turning away so she wouldn't have to see the dead man's hateful face. "Abrams disconnected it."

"Better hurry and get it online," Remy said, all grim authority restored to his tone. "We'll have company arriving... soon."

Chapter 9

LILLY

Lilly pushed her reluctant charges down the short corridor to the check-in station, where Deputy Pierce sat behind a thick, transparent security barrier, playing a holographic game. He bolted forward in his seat as they approached.

"Holy crap, Sheriff..." Pierce's faded blue eyes scanned Yercer's tall frame. "You got him?"

"Yep. Prime scum de la scum, Pierce. You catch the whiff from outside?"

"Sure did, boss." He grinned and buzzed them through.

"You're in way over your head, Sheriff," Yercer rumbled. "And your employees fooling around on the job. Tsk, tsk. What a shambles."

Lilly gave him an extra-hard shove for that. Pierce strutted out of the booth to help her. His counterpart, Potter, soon appeared and joined the convoy down to the cells. Neither deputy had seen much high-profile action in a while. She hoped they were still sharp. Both men were rapidly approaching retirement age, and Yercer had a nasty habit of escaping from even the most high-security establishments.

The cells were cramped, barred rooms designed for security rather than comfort. Each had a small, fortified window and an interior printed in one smooth piece—no joints, vents, cracks, or anything that could be exploited by enterprising inmates. All signals in or out were blocked. The beds and toilet facilities were as sparse as functionality permitted. The only concession to the prisoners' emotional needs was a view through each window.

Of course, a billboard currently blocked most of said view, but since criminal minds didn't typically coexist with well-developed souls, Lilly couldn't have cared less about the oversight.

Her deputies disconnected the linking chains between the four prisoners and shoved two of them into the first cell. Potter deftly removed their cuffs through the bars as per Naillik Security Regulations, Section 6. He then clicked open the next cell, but Lilly tapped her subordinate's arm.

"On second thought, I'll take Yercer with me. You look after this one."

"My pleasure." Potter prodded Yercer's sidekick into the cell.

Pierce led Yercer into an interrogation room, sat him down, and connected his cuffs to a bar in the middle of the table, forcing him to hunch his back. Not a terribly comfortable position, which was the whole point.

Lilly sat opposite him and stared at the big man. Pierce closed the door, handed Lilly a tablet, and then assumed the position of propping up the wall. Normally, she'd dismiss the deputy at this point, but somehow, she couldn't make the words come out.

Stony-faced, she scanned through several screens of info on Yercer's last known whereabouts and latest activities, none of which was new or surprising. She glanced up at him. "What are you doing in our town?"

"Sightseeing." He flashed her a mirthless grin.

"I'll repeat the question. What are you doing in our town?"

"Darlin'," he said with a labored sigh, "this ain't your town."

Lilly leaned in closer. "You all think I'm gonna just turn things over to you and your boss? You'd like that, wouldn't you?"

"What I'd like is irrelevant, my enticing, dark princess.

Like I said, you don't get it. Gono Darkbur has his fingers in everybody's pies." He eyed her up and down. "Soon, no doubt, in yours, too."

"Fingers can be so easily broken," Lilly replied with the utmost of calm. "Happens all the time in detention facilities, doesn't it?"

"Sure does, boss," Pierce helpfully answered from his corner.

"You're all pathetic," Yercer said. "Humans, dworgs, aflins, it don't matter the species... it don't matter the town. Sooner or later, you all fall in line. It's survival of the fittest, and darlin', those of us from Bane are pretty damn fit."

"If I didn't know better, Yercer, I'd think you were trying to impress me."

"Guess it wouldn't take much, huh? I remember your late husband."

Lilly's senses clouded in a haze of hatred for the man, the *thing*, sitting before her. "You're telling me that you and Gono already have footholds in Yerdua and Elocin?" Yes, it was on the nose. No, she didn't want to be in the same room with Yercer for any longer than necessary.

"We're everywhere. So, you see, little Miss Peace Officer, there's not gonna be much peace around here... from now on." Yercer's grin widened.

She pushed the button on the remote, sending an electric current into his body. He convulsed pitifully. But the yells she heard weren't coming from him. They came from just outside the room.

Lilly swung toward Pierce in confusion, but he looked just as perplexed as she was. She turned back to Yercer, who took a moment to compose himself.

"Why the hell did you do that?" he asked, a bit of spittle still stuck to the corner of his mouth.

"It's a sign of affection."

The door opened. Potter staggered into the room, a grimace plastered on his face.

Lilly sprang up from her chair. "What's wrong?"

"Forgot to switch off the restraints." Three sets of cuffs slipped from the deputy's hands onto the floor. "That hurt like hell."

Yercer started to laugh.

She hit the button again. The shock to his system sent him sprawling atop the table. This time, drool dripped from his mouth and worked its way to the floor.

Potter smiled when he saw that.

Lilly slammed one of the counterfeit nano-biotic packets down on the table, close to Yercer's thick nose. "The drugs are fake, but that's a real delivery packet. Now, who did you get the pretty wrappers from?"

There was a defiant silence. Even with his head still on the table, she could see the hateful smile begin to stretch across Yercer's broad face.

Her index finger hovered over the button, and she raised her eyebrows at him.

"Alright, alright," he said. "You wanna know the truth so bad, do you? Hell, I'll tell you. But don't say I didn't warn you."

"Yercer..." she said, her finger on the button now.

His eyes flashed to the remote in her hand. "Ducett... We got them from Ducett."

"Son of a bitch."

"Your brother," Yercer unnecessarily supplied—with such relish she wanted to zap him again and again until he passed out.

***

A few minutes later, with Yercer back in his cell, Lilly sat in her office, staring dully out the window.

Nate Ducett, her irresponsible younger brother, had arrived in Naillik shortly after she and Tim had moved here. And ever since, he'd been pulling one dumbass scheme after another. He was a con man, a criminal, but still her brother.

There was a sharp rap on the door.

"Yeah?"

The door opened, and Brand poked her head in, her blond mane swishing with excitement. "Sheriff, we had to arrest Ned Blakely."

Before Lilly could ask why, Brand added, "He stabbed Owen Carcell with a shucker knife."

"Huh. Just another afternoon at the Double L then," she said listlessly.

Ned shucked sand-oysters for the patrons at the Double L. Since seventy-five percent of the planet Vox comprised arid land, there weren't too many native species... at least not the kind you'd want to eat. Sand-oysters were the one and only that Lilly enjoyed. And the knife was meant for opening their shells, not gutting patrons.

"I put Ned in the back cell. He was pretty pissed off about something," Brand said.

"Guess he'd have to be... to stab someone."

Great, what else can possibly go wrong?

The planet's major crime syndicate was apparently trying to set up shop in her town. Her own stupid brother had dirty dealings with the bastards... and now, someone who Lilly had always considered level-headed had tried to shuck someone else.

The worst thing? The day was only half over.

Chapter 10

REMY

Remy hovered over Dreyla, whom he'd just promoted to chief engineer of the *Jay*. Basically, that meant she had the job of keeping the twenty-year-old ship in operation, and right now, she knelt in the engine room, attempting to undo what the mutineers had done to the *Jay*'s power.

"Protein bar?" Remy asked her, as he took a bite out of one.

She looked up, at first annoyed, but he could tell she was hungry. Smirking, he held up two bars: one yellow, one orange.

Dreyla scrunched her nose. "Which is less old?"

"Uh." Remy inspected the labels and handed her the yellow bar. "Banana flavor."

"Whatever that is."

Remy took another bite, chewed, and grimaced. "Our next loot better be food, like real food, the kind you get at the Atmogrille. Oh, them steaks with caramelized toro roots and a side order of mashed zarpa beans."

Dreyla smiled as she chomped gamely. "That would indeed be nice."

"Attention, R.L. Johnson," the comms system blared out. *"Stay powered down and prepare to be boarded."*

A weaselly male voice that sounded awfully familiar.

"What the hell?" Remy groaned. "Can't a man have his crappy dinner in peace?"

He shoved the last bite into his mouth, pulled Dreyla to her feet, and dragged her into the corridor, headed toward the bridge.

"We need to get this ship running," she protested, tugging him back toward the engine room.

"Might need you to help me with this first," he replied.

A minute later, they dashed onto the bridge, where Tosh was waiting for them—in Newman's recently vacated chair. Remy winced with regret: He'd miss his loyal, if whiny, gunner. The man had certainly deserved a better fate.

"Sounds serious," Tosh observed, drawing the captain's attention back to him.

After helping Remy move Joss's corpse to the cargo hold, the old man must've returned to the bridge. No patients, after all, awaited him in the medbay.

"Well, it ain't a party invite," Remy grumbled, taking his seat near the bow. "But fitting for the day we've had so far."

Dreyla raced to her nav station. "Looks like a command blade and two pirate ships off our stern." She frowned at her console. "Less than two minutes out."

"Tell me you're kidding." Remy pulled up the visuals on his screen.

Nope, she isn't kidding.

The command blade steadily approached, a menacing vessel four times the size of normal blades, and nearly as many times deadlier. He knew who was sitting in that ship. But what about the larger sidekicks flanking it? What asshats had chosen to side with Larker Max in this messed-up scheme to get rid of some perceived competition?

"Drey, what's the identity of the other two ships?"

"Already scanning," she murmured, eyes glued to the screen.

"I know that look," he said slowly. "I'm not gonna like the answer, am I?"

"No, Cap."

"Well, hit me with it anyway."

"It's the *Kapriano* and the *Mearle*."

"Damn." He slumped back in his seat.

The *Kapriano* was no surprise. Captain Langston hated his guts... on account of him sleeping with Langston's wife, Trinni, way back when. In hindsight, that little liaison hadn't been the most stellar of ideas, but man, *those legs*.

Langston's taste in ships didn't match his taste in women, that was for sure. The lumbering *Kapriano*, now identifiable in Remy's viewscreen, looked like a set of tin cans cobbled together, with copious weaponry strapped on to make it seem more imposing.

The *Mearle*, though. What a punch to the gut. He and Captain Pike—Jason the Red—had been *friends*. Or so he'd thought. Hadn't they pulled off half a dozen jobs together over the last decade and lived to laugh about it? That's what he got for trusting another pirate.

Jason's ship, the *Mearle*, resembled a cruiser from the front, all sleek lines and innocence, but a battleship from behind, with its badass array of missile heads and multidirectional heavy-duty blasters. Two-faced, just like its owner.

"*Attention*, R.L. Johnson," the voice ground out again. "*Under UNSF Code 4113, you are hereby charged with piracy. You are ordered to stay where you are and prepare to be boarded.*"

"Do you ever shut up?" Remy hit the comms button, but for audio only. "Sorry... currrrrrgh... we're having... currrrrrgh... difficulties... currrrrrgh... give us... currrrrrgh... couple minutes... currrrrrgh... clear it up." He switched off the mic.

Dreyla rolled her eyes at him, which made him smile—even though they were in yet another tight spot.

"*Attention,* R.L. Johnson," the voice repeated. "*Under UNSF Code 4113, you are hereby charged with piracy. You are ordered to stay where you are and prepare to be boarded.*"

"Like I'm gonna go quietly," he quipped.

"Cap, you don't do anything quietly," Dreyla said. "Anything."

It took him a second to realize what she was talking about. "How was I supposed to know that little redhead from customs was such a..." he started.

"Howler?" Dreyla offered, smiling.

Remy shrugged. "So, sue me," he said, winking at her.

"I think they intend to do more than that," she pointed out.

He'd been in tighter spots. Had more guns on him. Been backed into a corner. He wasn't worried... OK, maybe just a little bit.

Chapter
11
REMY

Remy stared down at the comms he'd just cut off, knowing his performance would only buy him, Dreyla, and Tosh a little time. He glanced at the screen displaying the three ships closing in on them, and then, he looked up into the eyes of his last two crew members. He needed to do what he always did: get them out of their current mess. Preferably alive.

"The both of you—get that power coupling reconnected. Fast!" Remy shouted. "My acting skills suck," he added under his breath. He'd used the sputtering *technical-difficulties* trick so often in his pirate career, he probably should've gotten better at it.

"What the hell do I know about power couplings?" Tosh

said, scratching his head.

"Come on." Dreyla marched Tosh off the bridge, tugging him along by the sleeve of his tunic.

Remy switched the comms setting to a different frequency, one he hoped the pursuing pirate ships would be monitoring. It was one thing for the United Nations Space Force to send a command blade after him, but for two of his own kind to have sided with the government, on behalf of a notorious crime lord with ties to the "right" people... well, that was just disloyal.

Of course, they were all pirates—himself included—and loyalty wasn't one of their most prominent virtues. Still, he wanted to see their faces.

The monitor flickered on, and he found himself staring at Jason Pike, the captain of the *Mearle*.

"Really, Jason?" he addressed the redheaded, mid-forties man, who was sporting a long beard—a new addition. "You're working with that bitch?"

The ginger beard rose a fraction with the disingenuous smile. *"Sorry, Remy, you know how it goes."*

"Larker's an idiot if he ever thought I was angling for his position."

"I told him that. But too many crews were starting to question his orders, turn down his jobs." Jason eyed him. *"Mostly because of your influence."*

"I never told anyone to follow me. I just don't take

kindly to having the feds on my ass."

The UNSF had doubled its presence in the Belt six months ago. Since then, Remy had strived to pull jobs less likely to ruffle any feathers, and thus keep flying longer. But this last gig was too lucrative to pass up.

He glanced at his external-view display. The command blade hovered menacingly nearby. Obviously, he hadn't been low-profile enough.

"Yeah, well, Larker didn't see it that way." Jason's gaze lowered. *"Sorry, man."*

"So you said." Remy clenched his jaw. "Out of idle curiosity, how large is that bounty on me?"

The other pirate captain sighed. *"A quarter billion."*

"Hard to turn down that kinda cash."

Jason didn't answer. Just preened his beard.

A quarter billion credits, even split between three crews, was a crapton of money. Enough maybe for a pirate to retire on. Hell, he could see why Jason had sold him out. It didn't make the guy any less of a bastard, though.

"Well, Jason the Red, it was good while it lasted," Remy said with a curl of his lip. "Watch your ass, though. Larker doesn't always keep his promises."

Jason leaned closer to the camera. *"Remy, if you want any of your crew to live through this, just do what she says, OK? Larker told her he wanted the ship and crew."*

Remy cocked an eyebrow. "But me...?"

"Yeah, uh, how she disposed of you was her choice."

"Well, I don't reckon she's gonna pamper me to death."

The pirate king Larker Max had played his hand well. He'd unleashed his UNSF attack bitch on the *R.L. Johnson*, confident her hatred for Remy would know no bounds. Her command blade, supported by two formidable pirate crews, would make it tough for even a skilled captain like Remy to escape the confrontation alive and unscathed.

Jason's shoulders tensed and his eyes darted nervously to the left. *"Crap, she's hailing me now... so, I... Remy, I... gotta go."*

"Do what you gotta do," Remy snapped, and then severed the link.

Do what you gotta do.

Fitting words. Jason the Red would always do what he felt he had to. The two of them were pretty similar, cut from the same tough pirate cloth. But how would Remy himself have acted if the tables were turned and it was Jason's head bearing such a massive bounty? Remy knew the answer: He wouldn't betray a friend for the sake of money, unless his own crewmates were at risk.

He hit the shipboard comms. "Any update on when we might have power?" he asked, all nice and polite.

"I need a couple minutes," came Dreyla's voice, ragged at the edges.

Poor girl was feeling the strain. But minutes were getting just about as scarce as loyalty in this accursed universe.

Chapter 12

DREYLA

"Damn. Seriously?" Dreyla said, her voice muffled in the tight, dark compartment behind the engine control panel.

It was suffocating in here, smelling of burnt rubber and hot as all hell. With so many wires running in and out of the system, she was having a tough time identifying the ones she needed.

Tosh's footsteps padded across the engine room. He stopped somewhere nearby. "What's wrong?"

She poked her head out so she could see him. Gulping a few breaths of cooler air, she wiped sweat from her hairline with her sleeve. "Abrams really did a number on this. Look, all the leads are ripped off." She held up a flexible, three-inch-wide tube containing over a dozen wires. "And it's difficult to tell what lines were spliced in where."

Tosh's watery slate-blue eyes widened as if he understood the damage, but then he shook his head. "I have no idea what you're talking about, but something tells me it's not good."

"You're right, it's not good." She picked through the wires, straightening them. "Remy needs this working an hour ago. These all need to be reconnected to power the converters. No connection, no reaction from the Teez... no power from the dark-matter generator."

Don't panic. You can do this.

She glanced at the old man to ensure he was OK, and still lucid. Of course, that judgment call wasn't easy to make, since Tosh's face was awash with its default, stoned expression. Even in the middle of performing complex surgeries, such as reattaching a hand or foot to one of the crew... he always wore the same dazed look. But damn, he was a good doctor. Tosh had mad skills; he just had a propensity for various addictions and a disregard for any local laws that might attempt to curtail his habit. Alcohol and narcotics were his primary vices. But what of it? People had much worse faults than that.

"What?" Tosh's eyes narrowed inquisitively, making him seem less vague.

She'd been staring at him. Zoning out. She shook her

head to clear it. "Nothing… I need you to run to the cargo hold and get the hand torch Abrams kept in his green toolbox. By the supply-room door. I need it to reattach these."

"Hand torch? Got it." Tosh trotted out of the engine room, as if happy to be useful for something.

She finished straightening the wires, separating the red, blue, and yellow so she could easily weld them to their correct plates when she got the torch. She crawled back behind the panel where the air seemed hotter than before. Sweat ran down her face in rivulets now.

Just as she'd fastened the wires in place with little metal pins, Tosh's head poked around the corner.

She jumped, banging her head on the ceiling of the compartment. "Whoa, nearly gave me a heart attack!"

"That's OK, I'm a doctor." Tosh grinned down at her.

While the old man was perhaps the kindest person she'd ever met, he still had a scary face, even when he smiled—or *especially* when he smiled. The deep lines of age, the sunken leathery cheeks, and the wiry eyebrows conspired to make him seem rather forbidding. It didn't help that he was now flushed from his sprint to and from the cargo hold.

As she grabbed the torch from him, she noticed he was cradling one of the TZ107 chips in his other hand. That single Teez chip could power the *Jay* for six months, and there were currently fifty thousand of the infernal things in the cargo hold. They'd stolen them on a job for Larker Max, the same pirate king now trying, via his ruthless minions, to double-cross them.

"Too bad we can't send a package of these over to those ships and blow the hell outta them," Tosh remarked with a rueful smile.

She nodded impatiently and turned her focus to the job. But a few seconds later, she stopped mid-weld and stared at him. She reached out and grabbed his forearm with her free hand, clutching tight.

"What?" the old man asked, his eyebrows at full tilt.

"You're brilliant!" Dreyla said, laughing.

"Well, if you say so," Tosh said. "But... maybe remind me why?"

Instead of answering him, Dreyla tapped her comms. "Captain," she blurted. "Don't tell them that Joss and Abrams are dead. Tell them you're in the middle of a mutiny... that should give you more time."

"What are you talking about?" Remy's voice was curt, his tone suspicious.

"Also, don't try to bring the power back online."

"But—"

"Trust me, we'll be there in a few minutes."

"But, Drey—"

"Please, Captain!"

She switched off the mic and met Tosh's startled gaze. No time to explain further—to either of them. Remy would likely give her an earful for that later, but he'd just have to trust her. Or else they'd all be in even deeper crapola.

Dreyla finished welding a red wire to its plate. She tested it with her meter to make sure the lines were connected, but she didn't bring the main power back online. Not yet.

Tosh looked at her quizzically, drumming his fingers against his whiskery cheek. "Did I miss something? I'm quite sure I must've. At my age, I do find it hard to keep up sometimes."

"We need to do a little surgery, Doc." She took his arm and guided him back toward the cargo hold.

This is gonna be gross.

Chapter 13

LILLY

Instead of swiping one of the patrol vehicles, Lilly set off on foot to the Red Lady. She needed some air. Despite the aridness of the planet and the mixed bag of odors in the overcrowded city, it was still better than being cooped up in her office, breathing in the processed air of the sheriff's station.

She worked her way down the crowded sidewalk. Trapped in her thoughts. Taking little notice of those around her. The encounter with Yercer had left her feeling queasy.

He was getting on her nerves, complaining about the view from his cell, demanding special meals due to his "dietary requirements," and ruthlessly teasing the weakest link in the chain of command: Deputy Brand. Luckily, Davis was in protective mode around his new colleague, fighting back whenever Yercer got too nasty. Otherwise, Lilly couldn't have left the station at all.

The six-story facade of the Red Lady cast a long, cooling shadow across her path. It was around this time of day when she and Tim had first arrived in Naillik—when the shadows lengthened and the sunlight bathed everything in a pinkish-orange glow. Romantic colors, for people who were inclined that way. She and Tim weren't.

Tim had been all fired up about his new job. He'd gotten hired by the main council from the planet Naillik, the home world of humans and the town's namesake. In those days, she and her husband felt they'd discovered the secret to happiness: a decent job on a planet boasting an enormous mining boom.

Yep, we were young and stupid.

Two years in, they'd become more realistic. Money was tight, and the town was showing its ugly side, but they still had ambitions. When Tim came home from work one day and convinced her to buy a stake in the Red Lady, she'd admittedly had her doubts. But the saloon-hotel-brothel combination was ultimately a solid investment. Plus, the purchase had allowed them to take up residence there—a better option than the three-hundred-square-foot apartment the council had originally provided.

Lilly ran her fingers along the porous outer wall. The faded red had once been bright and lavish—a feature Tim had reinstated after buying his share in the business. The previous owners had failed to maintain key aspects of the building, and now, without her husband's work ethic, she'd become equally slack in her duties.

Thanks to such neglect, the Red Lady seemed less respectable these days. A year of harsh sunlight and wind-whipped sand had taken its toll.

As she stared at the weathered exterior, she could easily imagine Tim's disapproving voice: *"Look at the state of the place. It's just laziness, Lilly, that's what it is. Civilization starts with maintaining things, showing that someone cares."*

Sorry, hon. Gotta choose my battles.

Lilly stepped through the main entrance into the relative gloom of the lobby. A heady, spicy aroma hit her nostrils, clearing her sinuses of any lingering odors from the streets of Naillik.

Billings, one of her business partners, lounged behind the counter at the center of the room, talking into his headset. He was the one who'd convinced Tim to invest in the joint. In all likelihood, he'd hoped that partnering with the sheriff would keep out the riffraff and prevent having to pay off the law for any violations the establishment might incur. After all, Tim *was* the law.

Smart move.

Billings was middle-aged and in reasonable shape. Any bodily imperfections he might have had were camouflaged by a crisp, dark suit. Lilly had never seen him in anything else.

"Robert." Lilly stepped closer, aware she was leaving a trail of sand on the polished floor.

Never mind. The bots'll get it.

He nodded and offered her a genuine smile, showing off his straight teeth.

By the sounds of the conversation, he was in the middle of a difficult negotiation with a hotel guest. He offered her an apologetic shrug.

Lilly signaled *OK* with a wave and slipped past. He would have engaged in more conversation if he'd been free to chat, but honestly, she wasn't in much of a talking mood.

After Tim's death, many of her employees believed that the two of them would end up together. Robert was a good guy and all, but he wasn't her style.

Maybe she just didn't have a style anymore.

Lilly headed through the saloon doors. She was still on the clock and wanted answers.

Just as her boot stepped onto the glossy blue floor, she spotted Reanda behind the bar. The female dworg was her other partner in the Red Lady. She had signed on to run the saloon and the brothel. No mean duty for someone who was only three and half feet tall, but like the men of her race, she had powerful muscles and an impressive beard. The muscles helped her maintain order with the customers, and the beard, which she kept braided, added to her general aura of badassery.

Lilly had once witnessed Reanda lift and toss a full-grown human male through the saloon's front window. A costly repair, but the guy had had it coming, and the incident had established Reanda's reputation as someone not to be messed with.

Naturally, the diminutive dworg had her soft side, too. She mothered the working girls, who could all count on her to keep them safe and happy in a profession that rarely offered such guarantees.

Reanda slid down from her perch behind the bar—a custom-designed shelf allowing her to keep an eye on things from an elevated position—and folded Lilly into a bear hug. Even though she only came up to Lilly's chest, her embrace still felt all-encompassing.

In essence, the dworg mothered her as well.

"Heard you ran into some of Darkbur's men." Reanda released her and took a step back. "You gotta be careful dealing with that scum, Sheriff."

"We had it under control." Lilly fought to keep defensiveness out of her voice. "But you're right about the scum part." She scanned the room. "Speaking of... have you seen my brother?"

Reanda squinted. "What's he done now?"

"Plenty."

She shook her head and sighed. "Haven't seen him. Sorry."

Reanda shifted her gaze toward the far gambling table where several patrons were playing Crimson Eight, a tricky game using eight-sided dice with ambiguous rules that, after all her time in Naillik, Lilly still didn't quite grasp. Of course, all that mattered to her bank account was that it favored the house.

"Teal," Reanda called in a voice that sliced through the air.

A tall, slender aflin turned away from the game he was running and acknowledged his wife's call with a single upward nod. Given that dworgs and aflins originally hailed from two separate planets and that the contentious races had waged several wars during the past, everyone was surprised by their relationship. Apparently, true love had no limits.

"Yes, darling?" Teal asked in a thin, wavering tone that

76

seemed to suit him.

As far as Lilly knew, the only conflict the inter-species couple had ever had was whether they would learn each other's language. Neither was easy to master, or even to speak passably. In the end, they'd opted to stick with the common dialect, which, luckily, they both knew. Lilly couldn't remember the last time she'd heard either of them speak their native tongue.

"You seen Nate?" Reanda asked as he approached.

"What's he done now?" Teal asked in exactly the same manner his wife had done seconds ago. But then, noting the frustrated look on Lilly's face, he answered, "No, haven't seen him, but Tryst is upstairs. Maybe she knows where he is."

"Which room?" Lilly asked.

Reanda scanned through a small display by the bar. "410... want me to come up with you?"

"No, thanks, I got this." Lilly patted Reanda on the shoulder and smiled at Teal, then headed for the elevators.

Chapter 14

SHAW

Commander Tara Shaw clicked her silver fingertips rapidly against the console. "He's claiming their comms are damaged," she muttered in as neutral a tone as her acting talents allowed.

"And you believe that?" Larker Max asked. Onscreen, her boss cocked his egg-shaped head at her, creating an effect every bit as irritating as in real life.

"I stopped believing anything Remy Bechet says right about the time he took my arm."

Her gaze trailed to her right arm, now a mechanical replacement. She flexed her fingers. It was the strongest arm money could buy—Larker's way of putting her deep in his pocket—but it didn't feel the same as the left one and never would. How many times had she dreamt that she had her old arm back and then awoken to twist her head on the pillow and see the prosthetic one instead?

"Give him enough time and that scumbag can get himself out of anything," Larker said, in a thinly veiled attempt to rile her further.

"If you'd listened to me," she replied, tilting her chin up, "I could've taken their ship at Yertie Commons."

"You have your orders. Get me that cargo, and their ship, but no matter what, Captain Remy Bechet dies."

The screen blanked out. Larker had cut off communications.

No matter what.

She liked those three little words much more than all the chitchat that had already taken place. She'd try, maybe not very hard, to capture the ship and its cargo intact. But no matter what, she was killing Bechet.

Shaw rose from her seat and paced around the small bridge.

Damn Larker Max with his superior attitude and orders.

Who was he anyway? Just a pirate king of delusions.

She curled her artificial fingers into a fist, imagining the damage it would do to Larker's long, sallow face. In many ways, the prosthetic was better than the original—a fact that Bechet didn't fail to point out a year after blasting it off with a plasma rifle.

"Looks like you got a better one," he'd said. He was charming like that.

The memory from that original encounter nearly five years ago was still fresh and painful. She had nabbed that little brat of Bechet's and promised to let her go if he just surrendered. (That was back in the days when she wasn't on Larker Max's payroll.)

The girl had overheard Shaw telling the snipers to take the shot as soon as Bechet was in range. But they hadn't gotten the chance. The pirate's crew had found their locations and taken them all out.

"Lieutenant..." Bechet had asked as he approached, searching for her name.

"Shaw," she'd responded.

"I just want the girl. Nobody else needs to get hurt here," he'd said.

A total lie.

When she'd threatened to slit the girl's throat, he'd raised his rifle and shot her arm poised with the blade. His blast had ripped through the flesh and bone of the appendage—something the medics explained later. At the time, she had lost consciousness. The blast had also caught her in the chest but hadn't penetrated her armor plating. If it had, she would have been dead.

Now, all she had to show for it was a robotic arm and a very different career.

"Commander, I'm detecting some damage around their communications array," Officer Zain said from his station at the far corner of the bridge.

Zain pointed to the monitor offering a clear scan of their quarry. The *R.L. Johnson* had sustained considerable damage but still seemed reasonably intact.

"Don't be a fool," Shaw said in the cool voice she reserved for underlings.

As Zain's chiseled face fell, Shaw looked away, remembering when she, too, had been an eager officer, keen to prove herself. She'd been on the fast track to management level, having aided in taking down half a dozen pirate crews—until she'd been forced to spend three months in rehab getting used to her new arm. That time had cost her.

She would make Bechet pay the toll.

On her port and starboard displays, the two support ships that Larker had sent to chaperone her gamely held their positions.

She had strongly objected to their participation in this caper, especially the *Kapriano*, as she knew Captain Langston hated Bechet almost as much as she did—thanks to some pitiful argument over Langston's wife.

But Shaw wanted her revenge. No pirate with a pathetic chip on his shoulder would deprive her of the pleasure intended to be hers and hers alone.

"Commander, is it true they have half a billion credits' worth of Teez on board?" Officer Jibs asked, a glint of dollar signs flashing across his eyes.

And there it was—the real reason Larker had sent the two pirate ships. No doubt her boss trusted that her hatred for Bechet would ensure the captain's demise, but half a billion was an awful lot of money. Larker's faith clearly didn't extend to her coming home with the goods.

Guess he isn't a fool after all.

"That's right, Jibs. Fifty thousand chips, worth half a billion credits."

Jibs wasn't the sort to rise more than two ranks in the UNSF hierarchy during his next sixty years of service. A total dullard by many people's reckoning. But at least he wouldn't have the imagination or the guts to double-cross her.

"What about these two?" Zain asked.

He, conversely, was an altogether more promising officer, if irritating at times, and someone she'd have to watch.

"Once we have confirmation that Bechet is dead and we have the cargo and crew, we kill the rest of them," Shaw said. "The universe could use less pirate scum."

"And Larker Max?" Jibs exchanged a nervous glance with Zain.

Shaw examined her silver prosthetic fingers and let a long and meaningful silence draw out before answering. "To hell with him."

The young officers failed to suppress their smiles—the kind of greedy smirks that only dreams of infinite wealth could bring. The carrot was firmly in place. There wouldn't be any trouble from these two while she conducted her mission.

Of course, she knew her underlings had discussed this possibility between themselves on the trip out, and no doubt well before that point. They were aware of her reputation. She had been taking pirate payoffs for years now, and that information had leaked out to the right people. She had done some unscrupulous, even downright villainous deeds, and officers in desperate need of extra cash—or extra adventure—caught on pretty quickly.

Hell, I might as well be a pirate.

Pirates, after all, had a very simple code: kill or be killed. And always exact revenge when it's deserved.

Chapter 15

DREYLA

Dreyla and Tosh had reached the cargo hold. So far, the old doctor was cooperating, if only with a bewildered *damned-if-I-don't* kind of vibe. Her plan was crazy as all hell, Remy was probably imploding with frustration up there on the bridge, but the adrenaline pumping through her veins kept her limbs moving on course.

Stopping to explain would take too long, not that it would help any. Remy would just say *no*, deeming her plan too risky, and the captain had had enough insubordination to deal with today.

She dragged Tosh by the arm over to Abrams' lifeless form sprawled in the center of the hold.

"Whoa, slow down, girl." Tosh raised his palms and patted the air. "You want to what?"

"Pack a hundred Teez chips into him... and this." Dreyla held up a device roughly the size of a half-loaf of bread.

A streak of blood trickled from Abrams' face onto the deck. She felt nothing for the dead man. Same with Joss, whose body lay nearby. They both deserved their sticky end.

Brinx and Newman were a different story, but she couldn't focus on them yet. She had a job to do. Her gaze drifted back to Abrams. The dead mechanic was just a prop in her plan now, nothing more.

Tosh tugged the device from her and twisted it in his hands. "Is this what I think it is?"

"Yep. A small dark-matter reactor wired to a short-range receiver."

She knelt onto the deck and pulled Abrams' shirt open, exposing his flabby stomach. The sight of his pallid skin, with its smattering of curly brown hair, disgusted her.

She looked up. Tosh's wide eyes fixated on her face.

"We need to plant all of this in his gut and then dress him again," she explained.

"You're turning Abrams into a bomb?" Tosh's voice was faint. "This is your plan?"

She grimaced. "Come on, Doc. We ain't got time for this. He's dead. And you look like a med student at his first dissection. Besides, I got the idea from you."

"That'll teach me to think out loud." Tosh shook his head and hunkered down on the other side of the body, his gaze darting between the dark-matter reactor and the man's white stomach, as if calculating how best to fit Exhibit A into Exhibit B.

Dreyla unsheathed her knife, flipped it over, and offered it to him. She nearly sagged with relief as he pulled it from her fingers.

"Wait 'til Remy hears about this," Tosh growled.

"Reckon if I keep him alive, he won't mind so much."

Hell, Abrams had been a mutineer, so the captain wouldn't care if she just released the corpse out into space and used it for target practice with the *Jay*'s rear guns.

Tosh held her gaze. "OK, but just a warning, Abrams always ate like a pig. No telling what's gonna pour out when we remove his guts."

"Hey, we all been eating the same protein bars. How weird can it get?" Still, she gagged a little at the thought.

"Well, it ain't gonna be rainbows, missy."

Tosh gave her a *last-warning* look before positioning the knife at Abrams' sternum and sliding it down the torso in a long incision. The first few seconds were OK. The thin dark-red line was precise, almost artistic.

But she wasn't prepared for the stench that followed, and the horrifying way the dead man's bloody, balloon-like innards spilled slickly to the floor as Tosh pulled them from the corpse. She shrank back, covering her lower face with her arm, afraid to swallow. She fought her instinct to back the hell off and find a distant corner to puke in. On a distant ship. In a distant galaxy.

Maybe disgusting crap like this explained why Tosh was perpetually stoned.

"Why don't you get the device rigged up to the chips? I got this," Tosh said in a gentle voice.

Dreyla nodded, and stole another look at the body, morbid fascination still rooting her to the spot.

She rose shakily and moved as far away as she could get in the cargo hold, but it didn't feel far enough. Swallowing hard, she hooked the Teez chips up to the dark-matter reactor and tried to ignore the squishy sounds coming from the center of the room. Each splash made more of the blood drain from her face. Each splatter sent another pang of queasiness from her stomach to her throat. They weren't sounds she wanted to associate with the human body... even a piece of scum like Abrams.

Dreyla soldiered on, swallowing bile, thanking her lucky stars she'd never opted to study medicine. Not that she'd had the choice, having been raised in a slave colony on Dihous Four. Having never known her parents—much less if they'd given her up willingly—she had only left that highly illegal hellhole when she'd been sold to the mining outfit on Kofax Prime, one of the largest rocks in the Belt.

She always laughed whenever someone mentioned how slavery had been abolished on Earth (or at least in Remy's home country) two centuries ago. In truth, some UNSF officials knew about the slave operations, but they'd just chosen or been paid to look the other way. Humanity still sucked as bad as it ever had.

"I'm all done, Drey," Tosh announced some minutes later, just as she'd finished with the Teez chips.

She returned to the bloody mess on the cargo-hold floor. Abrams' torso had been hollowed out, leaving a liquid hole where his guts should've been. She had witnessed men being killed, and even some uber-gross spectacles, like an arm being blown off someone... but this was far worse. The deck now resembled one of those old horror films Remy used to watch with her. The ones where zombies ate people alive.

Course, he's dead. Can't feel a thing.

Tosh's face creased with grandfatherly concern.

"We don't need to sew the body back up," she explained quickly. "We just need enough room to get an enviro suit on him."

Since the suits were skintight, a giant handmade bomb wouldn't fit unless it was inside the body. And the suit was key to her plan. After setting the timer, she handed Tosh the reactor but hung on to the converter lines tied into each individual chip.

"Hate to be pedantic, but isn't that enough Teez to blow up... well, all of us?" Tosh asked.

"Trust me," Dreyla said.

She winced in ridiculously empathetic pain as Tosh adjusted the device inside Abrams' cavity, but she held it together enough to hand him the chips and the lines, which were all still attached to the reactor. Hopefully, the depravity of this plan would prevent anyone from seeing through it.

"The reactor isn't strong enough to convert the energy required to blow us all up," Dreyla assured the old man. "At least... I hope."

Tosh halted his stuffing. "You... hope?"

"It-it'll work. We'll be OK. Now let's get the enviro suit on him and, uh, grab one of the shielded helmets."

Tosh raised a wiry eyebrow.

"I don't want them to see his face," she explained.

"Oh, yes, that gutted expression of his," Tosh murmured. "Off-putting, isn't it?"

Dreyla couldn't even manage a smile. Her head spun with the sheer number of things that could go wrong. The command blade had every kind of sensor and camera on board; the Shaw woman and her minions would be checking everything.

Well, maybe not everything. It's our only hope.

"So, we put him in the airlock with the Teez shipment and release it all?"

Tosh's deadpan tone didn't give any hints as to his assessment of their chances, and that was fine with her. She didn't want to know. Even if it was stupid and suicidal, it was better than doing nothing. Of course, that was precisely what she'd asked Remy to do—nothing. Any second now, he'd sprint into the cargo hold, demanding an explanation.

She looked up at Tosh and let her gaze linger on his face, which made him cock his head at her curiously.

"What?" he asked. "You stealing my ideas again, girl? This time, I didn't say nuthin'."

"You need a hat," Dreyla said.

Tosh rolled his eyes, his fingers grappling the pocket where he kept his stash of dope. "I don't dare ask what for."

Chapter 16

REMY

Remy stood over the nav station, squeezing and flexing his fingers. If they ever got out of this alive, he was going to flay that girl. His instincts screamed at him to power up and run. Between his flying skills and Dreyla's navigation prowess, they'd have a fifty-fifty chance. But the nav station still showed the main engines doing a big, fat load of nothing.

Why had she asked him to stall? And why the hell had he done nothing to stop her?

Whatever she's got planned, it better happen soon.

Those three ships were creeping closer, and they didn't

look any friendlier the nearer they got. He didn't want them to reach umbilical range.

A commotion from the corridor made him turn.

Dreyla dragged Tosh onto the bridge. But this was a Tosh that Remy had never seen before. He had two large blades strapped to his chest. He carried a double-barreled blaster as if he knew how to use it. His face and clothes were drenched in blood. And strangest of all, perched on top of his head, was a black pork pie hat with a red feather.

Remy pointed at the doctor. "Hey, that's my hat."

"Remy, meet the *Jay*'s new captain," Dreyla said with a smirk.

Tosh gave a goofy wave. "Sorry about the hat, Captain."

Another warning crackled through the comms. This time accompanied by a large plasma beam blasted across the *Jay*'s bow.

Remy gazed down at the nav console, noting the encroaching enemy ships on the display, then glanced back at Dreyla, one eyebrow cocked quizzically.

Dreyla stepped toward her station and pushed him aside. "Captain, there's no time to explain, but if this is gonna work, you need to keep outta sight." She slid into her seat and brought up the display for the ship's main reactor as well as a secondary reactor.

The steel-like urgency of her tone prompted him to move his ass over to Newman's former station, just as Tosh stepped closer to his.

Over the past eight years, Remy and Dreyla had pulled a lot of jobs together, and he'd taught the girl everything he knew about being a pirate. He'd shown her that a job didn't always demand the attack-and-conquer approach. If at all possible, he preferred doing it nonviolently, conning his way in and out of sticky situations. He wasn't afraid to fight, but stealing and bolting often guaranteed a better chance of keeping him and his crew alive.

Needless to say, Larker Max favored the old-fashioned way: kill and take what you want. Based on the situation, and whatever scheme Drey had set up, it seemed as though she was following in Remy's footsteps: con and flee.

Secretly, he beamed, ever the proud father.

Tosh activated the video and audio comms to respond to Commander Shaw. Remy chuckled inwardly, imagining how her temper had heated to white-dwarf levels at being made to wait. If the circumstances weren't so serious, he might actually enjoy the show.

"Who the hell are you?" Shaw snapped.

"I'm Captain... Captain Robert Tosh," the old man said amicably.

"And who made you captain?" Shaw narrowed her green eyes to slits. *"That weasel Bechet?"*

"Actually, you did, when one of your mutineers killed him a few minutes ago." Tosh had continued his amiable tone with a remarkable poise that Remy could only admire.

"Killed him? Abrams and Joss killed Bechet, is that what you're telling me?" Her greed for the truth made her voice all kinds of screechy.

"We've been fighting them for the last twenty minutes. After Abrams knocked out our power, Captain tracked him to the cargo hold. Killed the scum." As Tosh continued to spin his tale, a note of cold menace entered his tone. "But Joss, the coward, managed to slip away for a while, set a trap, and shoot Captain Bechet in the back."

"Where's Joss then?" Shaw asked. *"Why hasn't he contacted me?"*

"Because, *Commander*, I rammed a twelve-inch blade through his throat."

Remy leaned over the console and examined the side of Tosh's menacing face. The old man's craggy features looked downright livid, an emotion the captain had never observed in him before. Given his aging, rockstar-like fitness, sinewy muscles, and pointed expression, someone could actually mistake him for a fierce pirate.

"You killed him?" Shaw's delicate nose scrunched with incredulity, but a new understanding dawned in her eyes.

"And now, I am captain of this ship." Tosh straightened his posture against the captain's seat with a natural ease that made Remy smile.

"Fine," Shaw snapped, clearly rankled at having been

robbed of the pleasure of killing him herself.

Course, she might still get that chance.

She glared at Tosh. *"Prepare to be boarded."*

"I don't think so," Tosh said, and before she could protest, he added, "I get that you wanted the man dead. And I get that you want the cargo. I'm prepared to give you both, but after that, we'll be on our way."

There was a heavy silence. It reminded Remy that only the ambience-control system was running, not their engines.

"No." Shaw's voice hardened to its full, vicious power. *"We will board you, take the cargo, and then decide whether or not we wish to let you live."*

Her trademark, closed-lipped smile appeared—one that turned weaker men to quivering idiots. But the doctor was no such man.

"Commander," he said, with a hint of forbearance, *"I'm prepared to scuttle this ship—an action that will leave your boss, Larker Max, upset. Some might say very upset."*

Remy watched as another image popped up alongside Shaw's. Langston's scrawny face.

"Where's the body?" Captain Langston yelled.

"Langston, I told you to keep off the comms," Shaw hissed.

Langston and Shaw started arguing. It was clear the

96

commander's patience had worn thin with the pirate. After a few sparring rounds, she ordered one of her officers to block all communications coming from the *Kapriano*. Diplomacy never had been her strong suit.

"As much of a pain in the ass as he is, Langston does have a point," Shaw announced with a toss of her blonde head. *"I want to see Bechet's body."*

"We will send it out through the starboard airlock, along with the shipment of Teez. Your guys can pick up both, and then we'll all be on our way," Tosh said, all cooperation personified.

Remy glanced toward the nav station and saw a grin creep across Dreyla's face.

Shaw pressed her own face closer to the camera. *"When I see his dead body, we will discuss what the future of the* R.L. Johnson *is. Then and only then."*

"Release the body with the cargo," Tosh demanded of no one in particular.

Remy assumed that Tosh and Dreyla had already loaded both into the airlock. There was a chance this crazy-ass plan, one that Remy had figured out only a moment ago, might have some merit after all. It certainly had style, and a feathered hat to boot.

"Both are loaded, Captain," Dreyla said from off to the side, her hands clenched over two different panels, ready to make her move.

Hearing her address the old man as "Captain" like that made Remy chuckle. He stifled the sound when Tosh broke character to glance back at him. After an instant, the old man snapped back to his pretense as the captain.

"Open the airlock," he commanded.

Through his gunner display screen, Remy watched as a large pallet of Teez and a disguised body, which he assumed was Joss or Abrams, floated out through the starboard airlock and drifted into the vastness of space.

"As soon as you intercept them, we'll be on our way," Tosh said. Then he shut down the comms.

Remy rose to greet him, arms spread wide. "Tosh, that was an award-winning performance. The last line was maybe overkill, but I think we got her, you old devil." He patted a spot on the doctor's shoulders that wasn't as blood-soaked as the rest of his outfit.

Tosh stumbled back, the familiar dull, stoned look washing over his face. "My mother always wanted me to go into theater."

"But you rebelled and became a doctor?" Snickering, Remy slipped into his station. He slid his fingers along the controls, assured that Dreyla's plan had played out perfectly. He turned to her. "I'm assuming that body belongs to one of our mutineers and that it's loaded with explosives?"

She nodded, her posture proudly erect. "It's Abrams."

Remy smirked. "Guess the bastard turned out to be useful, after all."

Dreyla's brown eyes darkened with apprehension. "Just hope it works."

He had taught his daughter well, but she was still finding her footing when it came to self-confidence, a prime requisite for being a good pirate, or at least surviving as one.

"Me, too," he replied, then, noting her furrowed brow, added, "Well, we better power up... and get ready to blow this popsicle stand."

"A popsicle sounds good right about now," Tosh murmured, wandering toward the exit.

"Whatever you say, Captain," Remy said, swiveling his chair away from the console.

Tosh winked at him before vanishing into the corridor.

Dreyla's gaze drifted toward the open doorway. "I don't know how he managed to keep it together."

"Course he did. He's wearing my lucky hat."

A grin transformed her face, bringing back her carefree youthfulness. "Can't believe we pulled it off, Remy."

"We haven't pulled off anything yet," he reminded her. But he couldn't fight his own grin.

He swung back to his controls and, once the power converters had kicked in, brought the piloting station and guns back online. And then ever so slowly, he used the lower landing thrusters to move away from the command blade and the two pirate ships. The thrusters wouldn't register to the human eye; he just wanted the ship to look like it was drifting.

But looks could be deceiving. This drifting had purpose, and with any luck, the low-powered thrusters would push them away from what he suspected was going to be a rather large explosion.

Chapter 17

LILLY

Lilly marched down the fourth-floor corridor in the Red Lady's brothel wing, which was separated from the hotel by dense, soundproofed walls and security doors. Here, the decor was dark and sumptuous—crimson walls and golden light fixtures. She didn't visit this part too often. But she needed to now, if only to talk to Tryst and finagle her brother's whereabouts out of her.

Within the brothel itself, the soundproofing wasn't nearly as effective. Maybe it was deliberate. Moans, murmurs, and heavy breathing emanated from the rooms—a cacophony of desires, mingling so well you couldn't tell which room had produced the sounds.

A sharp crack punctuated the ambience. She whirled around, reaching for her blaster, then realized it was just a whip.

Huh. Just a whip.

Seconds later came the inevitable cry of pain. A young male's voice. She shuddered, then moved on. As a stakeholder in the Red Lady, she should be totally at ease with the dominance-submission scene, and ethically, she was. She just couldn't get her head around asking someone to inflict pain, let alone begging for it.

Lilly reached her destination: Room 410. Hopefully, Tryst wouldn't be in the middle of something intimate, or worse. She cocked her head to listen, but no sound emerged. Not so much as a snore. In a brothel, no noise almost always meant trouble.

She pulled out her pistol and rapped on the door. "Tryst, open up. It's Sheriff Greyson."

No answer.

Just as she was about to force her way inside, the door inched open. A short, plump man in his fifties stood in the doorway, fully dressed in the kind of dark-maroon tux fashionable in the casinos of Elocin. He glanced down at Lilly's pistol, and his lips and chin trembled.

She holstered the weapon and looked down into his strangely babyish face. "Sorry, I thought there might be a problem."

As she brushed past him, he did nothing to stop her. At least he didn't think she was part of the act. That kind of misunderstanding had happened more than once, and it was always acutely embarrassing. For her as well as for the overeager patron.

"Do come in, Sheriff," a smooth voice crooned from inside the room. Tryst. Even when she was being polite, she sounded snarky.

The younger woman lay across a chaise lounge, preening her bright red hair. Dressed only in black panties and a matching lace bra, Tryst held Lilly's gaze brazenly with her bright blue eyes. She wasn't a model of human perfection, but her insolent, pixie-like charm, overlaid with an aura of sexual mischief, had worked its spell on many men—her brother, Nate, included. Formerly one of the most popular girls at the Red Lady, she had supposedly stopped taking clients once she'd started dating Nate. Or had she?

Tryst's legs stretched across the velvety chair, her feet propped on a pillow. Between each toe was a spacer. On the carpet before the lounge lay a toolbox containing all sorts of makeup and polishes. The heady ethanol waft of nail polish reached Lilly's nose. Tryst had apparently been enjoying a pedicure, nothing more.

"Billy, give me and the sheriff a few minutes." Tryst flapped her hand at the man still loitering in the doorway. "The polish needs to dry anyway."

He smiled and scuttled out, closing the door behind him.

Lilly raised an eyebrow. "Did I interrupt a tryst, Tryst?"

"Billy likes to paint my nails." Tryst wiggled her purple-polished toes and grinned impishly.

"So I see."

"That's *all* he likes to do."

"Yeah, maybe I'll get mine done, too. Have you seen Nate?"

Tryst moaned. "What's he done now?"

This standard response had gotten old. Maybe she should do something about that. More to the point, maybe Nate should do something. But the window of opportunity for her brother's character reform had probably closed long ago.

Lilly stepped nearer to the chair and adopted a casual smile she was pretty sure didn't fool the woman. "I just need to talk to him." She fiddled with the tassels of a lampshade and let an uncomfortable silence draw out between them. Oldest trick in the book.

Tryst tapped her big toenail to test if it was dry, leaned back again, and huffed. Her gaze darted over to Lilly, who merely returned the stare. Lilly had the advantage of time. She could stay here until the sun set, but Tryst undoubtedly had a full schedule of client sessions, and it would hurt her reputation to be late for the next one—if she was indeed back on the market. Besides, Billy Toenails was lurking outside the door, just dying to brush on a topcoat.

"It's about those nano-biotic packages, isn't it?" Tryst finally burst out.

"How interesting you should mention that," Lilly said.

Tryst pouted. "Look, I told him not to get involved with those guys, didn't I?"

"Those guys?"

"Well, I don't know, do I?" Tryst spread her arms. "He tells me nothing."

That rang of the truth.

Lilly nodded. "Not even that he's involved with Yercer Taul?"

Tryst swung her feet down onto the floor. "Taul? You're kidding."

"You didn't know?"

"He told me it was just a couple of small-time hoods. Figured they'd get themselves busted and that would be that."

"He *expected* them to get busted?" Even by Nate's twisted standards, this was unforeseen.

"Well, yeah, he didn't want them actually selling the stuff to people, did he? Just wanted them to pay him for the empty packaging. Said they weren't from here and that they didn't know what they were doing."

Yep, that was exactly the kind of half-assed, cowardly justification her brother excelled at. He couldn't even be properly bad.

There was a nervous tap on the door. Billy poked his head back inside.

Tryst held up her hand and waggled her fingers playfully. "Just a couple more minutes, honey," she cooed in a much sweeter tone.

Lilly admired her acting ability.

Billy simpered and retreated into the hallway.

"Why do you stay with Nate?" Lilly asked. "He's my brother, and even I think he's nothing but trouble."

Tryst's expression grew vague. "Why does anyone stay with anyone?"

Lilly swallowed and told herself not to think about that—not to think about Tim. She had to concentrate. "So, where's he at now? And don't try to fool me, darling, cuz I know you know."

Tryst smiled sweetly. "Your place."

"Son of a bitch!" Lilly started toward the door but stopped and turned. "Do not call him. I want to catch the little jerk myself."

Tryst smiled enigmatically.

Lilly headed out the door, passing the diminutive man who seemed eager to return to Tryst's toenails.

As she stepped from the brothel end of the building into

the hotel section, she saw several people clustered around the elevators. Assuming they were heading down, Lilly elected to take the stairs.

She slipped into the stairwell and climbed two flights to the penthouse suites. A heavy-duty door secured the entryway leading to this level, preventing any disgruntled customer or other lowlife from breaching the premises. The scanner beside the door was keyed to handprint or I.D. card, the latter of which Lilly had left back at the station. She placed her palm on the scanner, and a bright blue line scrolled up, verifying her identity. A moment later, the door opened.

Her place was all the way down and around the corner. Though each of the Red Lady's partners lived in a suite, it had made more sense for the two operating owners, Robert and Reanda, to have more convenient locations, closer to the elevators and the stairs. Luckily, though, her penthouse offered the finest view.

As she headed toward her suite, unsettling thoughts swirled in her brain. Chastising her brother had grown tedious. So had her job as Naillik's sheriff. Sure, she held a respected position and was a reputable business owner, but still, she found herself living on Vox, a place where nobody was normal. Everyone was either damaged or working an angle—or painting freaking toenails. Even most of the so-called "good" people weren't easy to respect. Hustlers, the lot of them. A mining planet like Vox was a magnet for that type of person. She'd just never thought that would describe her.

And yet here she was. Still here. Even with Tim gone and little else binding her to the town but a sense of duty likely driven by nothing more profound than her overblown ego. This ball of sand shouldn't even be inhabited. If not for the mineral that now powered most of their galaxy, it would still be a forgotten, arid rock in an inhospitable backwater of space with very little atmo.

Just who am I kidding anyway?

Chapter 18

SHAW

Shaw stood by her console. She preferred standing, even in battle. The chair always conveyed a certain amount of weakness in her opinion. She stared at the forward display monitor, watching the scene unfold. A large, wrapped pallet gently floated their way—a gyrating cube punctuating the darkness of space. It was about the size of nine pressurized coffins packed together in stacks of three, much larger than the typical size of a Teez shipment.

Being this close to that much Teez made even her hardened head spin. Just a small amount was enough to power a medium-sized city back on Earth for half a year. Since the discovery of the substance itself, and the process to make it react with dark matter, it had been an energy game changer, and it had made the stuff so valuable that those out here in the Belt used it as hard currency. That cube alone was worth all the fuss and bother of dealing with Larker Max. But the real prize had been the thought of blasting a hole in Captain Remy Bechet.

Still, there was something wrong with this delightful scene. Notably missing was Bechet's dead body. Her blood turned cold.

"Where's—?" she hissed, but she had to swallow back her next words as the body came floating into view right behind the pallet. Just a damn parallax effect.

She rubbed the back of her neck with her flesh-and-blood hand, nodding impatiently at Jibs and Zain to carry on. She needed to calm down, not get so emotional where Bechet was concerned, but frankly, it pissed her off that she'd missed her chance of ending him herself.

The lights from the *Kapriano* lit up both the package and the corpse. The ghostly, bluish glow bounced off the shiny, gray metallic suit and helmet of Bechet's body, causing a flare to appear on her monitor.

"Commander, the *Kapriano*'s moving," Zain announced from his station.

"Damn Langston anyway," Shaw muttered. "Lock weapons on her."

110

"Everything?" Jibs asked.

"Everything." She slapped the comms button. "Langston, do not approach the package. I repeat, do not approach the package."

"Sorry, Commander," came Langston's unapologetic voice. *"I have my orders. Larker was real specific on the details."*

"Well, let me be *real* specific, too, Langston. Touch either the package or the body, and I blow the *Kapriano* out from under your greedy, interfering ass and into the next galaxy. Got that?"

"Uh, did you see that?" Zain cut in. "The *R.L. Johnson*'s moving. Jibs, do a—"

"No!" Shaw snapped. "Jibs, keep your attention on the *Kapriano*." She turned back to the comms. "Langston, you've been warned. The *Johnson* is mine. It's your choice. We can do this the easy way or the hard way."

"Commander, something's not right here." With a crackle of static, Captain Jason Pike's gruff voice joined the comms conversation.

Shaw groaned. "Oh, what now?"

"Hey, Langston, I'd back off if I were you," Pike said.

"Stay out of this, Pike," Langston shot back.

"Commander," Pike appealed to her. *"You know I'm right."*

She was beginning to suspect as much. "Jibs," she ordered, "scan that container. Look for any energy signals that could belong to a reactor."

The *Kapriano* continued to glide forward. And as Zain had said, the *R.L. Johnson* was slinking away. They must be using their landing thrusters to avoid producing any telltale energy output.

Smart.

"Negative on any reactor signature," Jibs said.

"We're moving in to intercept." With a click, Langston's communications line went dead.

Zain turned to Shaw with a pale face, blinking rapidly. "Commander, the *Johnson*'s power just lit up."

Shaw nodded, frowning in concentration. Something even worse was bothering her. "Why did they put a helmet on the body?" she mused aloud. If Captain Tosh were just sending out Bechet's corpse with the Teez, why rig him with an enviro suit?

Zain's eyes widened in simultaneous realization. "Oh, no!" He whirled around to his colleague. "Jibs, Jibs, scan the body!"

Langston's ship had almost reached the Teez package. The left side of the screen flashed orange as the *R.L. Johnson*'s engines flared up, and the ship rocketed away.

Shaw gasped. "Target the—"

Suddenly, the body exploded in a blinding, blue flash that obliterated her words and everything else on the screen. The deck shook violently. The impact from the explosion threw Shaw forward, causing her upper body to smash into her console.

That son of a bitch.

Steadying herself, she refocused on the forward viewscreen and saw that the *Kapriano* had been ripped in half. The explosion had apparently severed the bridge from the main engines and boosters. Debris spilled out from the gaping holes in each half and drifted off into space. No emergency shuttles seemed to have taken off. Electric arcs fizzed all over both sides, as if a fireworks party was in full swing. This would be Langston's last soiree, that was for sure.

And good riddance to him.

The fact that she was still breathing meant that her own ship was functional, although they'd no doubt sustained heavy damage. An enormous amount of Teez had just burst apart, after all.

Her officers were hugging their respective consoles, still recovering. The *Mearle*, now floating into view again, also seemed to be mostly intact. Pike would live another day. A pity he hadn't been closer to the bomb.

"Dammit," Shaw croaked, jabbing her finger at the *R.L. Johnson* on the main screen. "Zain, pursue that ship. Don't let it out of your sight for a second."

Zain, his pinched, angular face bathed in sweat, maneuvered them around the debris. The *Mearle* followed suit. The *R.L. Johnson* already had a head start, but with a little luck, they might still catch up.

The comms came back on, and she found herself looking directly into the face of the man she hated most in the universe.

Captain Remy Bechet grinned back at her. He looked very much alive for a dead man.

"I should have known," Shaw sneered.

"Seriously? You thought that lumpy body was mine?"

"Your body *will* be lumpy when I'm finished with you."

"Commander, cut your losses," Bechet said cheerfully. *"Face it, Larker Max was gonna screw you over. Why were you doing his bidding anyway?"*

The pirate was right about one thing: Larker Max was a diabolical snake. Shaw had never trusted the man—hence, why she'd planned to swipe the Teez for herself. But since that was no longer a possibility—due to her mortal enemy's shenanigans—only one mission mattered now.

She glowered. "Why are you even talking to me?"

"Don't be sore, Commander. Larker Max screws with everyone."

"That's not why I'm sore." Shaw flexed the fingers of her prosthetic hand and curled them into a fist. "It's a little more personal than that."

"Well, it's personal to me when you threaten my people," Bechet growled back. *"Two good men are dead, thanks to your bloody mutineers."*

Shaw glanced at the external-view display. They were catching up to the *Johnson*. Bechet might have been able to fire his engines, but with his ship newly powered up, he wasn't yet able to attain full speed. Soon, she'd be able to wipe that insufferable grin off his face.

"Then just give yourself up," she said. "And I'll let your remaining people go."

He ceased grinning. There was a moment of hesitation on his face, as if he were truly considering her offer.

Interesting. So, it isn't a bluff. He really does care about his crew.

Then his smile returned at full wattage. *"Nah."*

She let his flippant response hang there for a few seconds. Not that she expected him to capitulate, but she wanted to give him the chance to consider the folly of his actions before his inevitable demise. Her two officers sat at their stations with their heads turned to her, riveted and waiting.

"Jibs?" she said in a cool, steady voice, keeping the comms open so Bechet could have absolutely no misapprehension. "Prepare to fire everything we have as soon as they're in range. Everything."

"Yes, Commander," Jibs squawked.

"*Shaw, Shaw, Shaw,*" Remy drawled over the comms. "*You sure you want to do this? Don't make me take that other arm.*"

She clenched her robotic hand into a fist and punched it through the screen, sending a shower of glass and sparks all over the bridge, forcing both Zain and Jibs to duck down.

The comms channel transferred to an auxiliary screen off to the side where Bechet was grinning more broadly, if that were even possible. He knew he had gotten to her. Knew that he could push her buttons.

"*Does the UNSF have anger-management classes, or something like that?*" the pirate asked smugly. "*Cuz, jeez, lady, you got a temper.*"

"You have no idea," she responded through gritted teeth.

The pirate captain looked sideways and then back into the camera. "*This should be interesting. We've got full power now.*" He winked at her, and the screen went blank.

Chapter 19

REMY

"'Don't make me take that other arm,'" Dreyla quoted. "Well, that was harsh."

Remy glanced up from his console, where he'd been scanning the *R.L. Johnson* for damage. "That was me holding myself back, gentleman that I am."

Dreyla bit her lip and stared at one of her screens. "Shaw's ship is trying to close the distance. To get within blasting range." She met Remy's gaze. "She's really pissed at you. Maybe we should've tried to negotiate something."

"Yeah, like she tried to negotiate that large blade across your neck," Remy replied, then looked down, scrambling to recalibrate the ship's weapons, which had been knocked off-kilter due to the previous encounter. "Cuz that's how she does negotiation. Real to the point-like."

Silence from Drey's station. He glanced up again.

Her face tightened, then after a few seconds, she nodded. He hated to be the one to remind her of their first and nearly last encounter with Commander Tara Shaw, but sometimes, he needed to temper Dreyla's youthful optimism for her own self-preservation.

"You keep watch on the debris from behind." He indicated the rear-view displays that showed pieces of the former *Kapriano* hurtling through space, way too close for comfort. "I'll keep fixing this." He let out a sigh. "Auto-calibration's dead. Have to do it the hard way."

After a few minutes of tediously jabbing controls and checking connections, he added, "Damn, I wish we'd gotten them all with that clever bomb of yours." He gazed at her. "But you did a helluva job, little one."

She blasted debris in three rapid shots and cocked her head at him. "Don't call me that."

He grinned. "I forget sometimes. You could probably take me down in a fight."

She rolled her eyes. "Yeah, right."

"Don't underestimate yourself, Drey. Brains often beat brawn."

"So, you're not upset?"

"About what?"

"For keeping the plan secret. And for blowing up most of the Teez. It was worth a fortune."

His eyes softened. "Our lives are worth much more."

"Still..."

But Remy had turned back to his console, scanning a display of everything in the quadrant. It was getting a bit more crowded than he generally liked.

"Is it just me or do they seem to be catching up with us?" Dreyla asked.

"Yeah. Tea break's over."

"Did someone say *tea break*?" Tosh wandered back onto the bridge, a glazed look in his eyes. It was hard to believe the old doctor had posed as a badass captain just a little while ago.

"Doc, did you just shoot up?" Remy snapped.

Tosh held his gaze but only fleetingly. "Well, if we're gonna die, I might as well fly," he mumbled.

As he shuffled toward Newman's former seat with exaggerated care, he uttered a few more incoherent words, but Remy didn't have time to ask for clarification.

"Sit down and buckle up," he instructed. "This ride's about to get crazy."

He tapped the screen of his electronic tablet, and immediately, the blues guitar of Tab Benoit rang out on every functional speaker throughout the old pirate ship. Another of his favorites. Another gem that Dreyla probably despised.

This time, though, she said nothing, just hunched herself stiffly over her controls, refusing to look at him. Which naturally made him smile. Playing this album always reminded him of seeing Tab perform—once, long before the incident at Newton's Gate had changed the world forever.

The concert had taken place in New Orleans. Remy couldn't remember the name of the venue—just that the music was amazing.

Sadly, once the catastrophic explosion at Newton's Gate had occurred, resulting in the opening of various portals, New Orleans had been one of several cities on Earth that had mysteriously vanished. Regrettably, old Benoit had disappeared right along with her.

Hard to believe that was twenty years ago. A lot of crazy stuff had happened since then, but playing the classics allowed him to pretend he was still back there, in a simpler world, in a simpler time.

Just after the incident, he had joined up with a long-haul crew that transferred supplies out to the Belt. A month later, he had switched to a pirate ship and was in the life from then on.

"We're heading back to the edge of the Holcom Range," he announced.

While Newton's Gate lay between the Earth and its moon, the explosion had caused portals to appear all over the planet, all over the solar system, and, presumably, all over the universe. Some of them were always open, enabling a person (or a ship) to travel from one place to another—and back again. Sometimes, even one planet to another.

Remy had also heard of some that lead to alternate Earths, but he couldn't wrap his head around such a concept. What would the blues music sound like on an alternate Earth? Would there even be any blues?

Not that Drey would mind.

He glanced behind him, where Dreyla was still staring at her nav monitor. She looked up when she felt his gaze.

Worry lines appeared above her eyes. "You're not by any chance thinking about trying to maneuver through the field again?"

"Sort of," he said.

He didn't want to cross the deadly asteroid field twice in one day, but he couldn't avoid it completely. He needed to find the easiest path along the edge of the Range that led to one of the few portals he'd seen this far out in the Belt. A portal he intended to fly through, as he'd done once before.

In a fit of desperation about a decade earlier, he'd used it when he needed an escape route from a few pesky blades. Despite the foolhardiness of such a decision, he'd veered directly for the portal and, without hesitation, flown the *R.L.*

Johnson through the mysterious gateway. It could've taken him anywhere, but luckily, it had popped him out on the far side of the moon.

This was the real reason he'd instructed Dreyla to chart a less death-defying route through the Range (before the whole mutiny thing had thrown his plan off course). Once there, he knew how to locate the portal, which he now intended to utilize for their getaway. First, though, he had to shake Commander Shaw and his old pal Captain Jason Pike.

The mournful twangs of Tab's guitar continued to fill the bridge as Remy maneuvered around some large asteroids.

"That, uh, story about you flying the *Jay* through a portal..." Dreyla said, in a tone that indicated she could read his mind. Which she often could.

"Yep?"

"That wasn't just some ridiculous pirate's tale?"

"Nope."

"Oh, man, I remember that," Tosh piped up, then glanced at Dreyla. "Long before you were with us."

Dreyla swiveled her head from Tosh and then back to Remy. Poor girl looked exhausted and overwhelmed. She wouldn't be the one brainstorming any brilliant solutions this time.

It was his turn to come up with the crazy plan.

A bone-jarring shudder told him their pursuers had started firing again.

"Dreyla, switch to front view," Remy shouted, grasping his own gunner controls.

They were in range of the other two ships, but just barely, so by zigzagging the *Jay*, he managed to avoid the blasts... for the most part. The ship rocked back and forth several times with "minor" explosions, but she kept flying. And he couldn't ask more of her than that.

"Popped us out on the dark side of the moon," Tosh rambled, waving his hands in the air. "That was so cool."

Remy ignored him and returned fire on the enemy ships, tagging the command blade a couple times but not doing much to slow her down. There was little chance now of blasting Shaw out of the galaxy. All they could hope to do was survive long enough to reach the portal.

Tosh chuckled. "That was the name of a Pink Floyd album."

Remy shook his head, spraying droplets of sweat onto his console. The old man sure picked some awkward moments for his trips down memory lane.

"Pink what?" Dreyla twisted to look at Tosh.

"*The Dark Side of the Moon*," Remy cut in sharply. "An amazing album. By a band called Pink Floyd... but hey, maybe we can discuss it later. You know, when no one's shooting at us."

He pummeled the trigger a few times at Pike's wing and winced as the return fire missed the *Jay*'s starboard side by mere meters. Pike appeared every bit as keen as Shaw to blow them to smithereens.

Probably pissed about the Teez bomb.

Remy flashed Dreyla a smile, then continued to shoot while taking fire.

She must've detected the strain in his face because she shrank into her seat and asked in a soft voice, "Are we gonna make it?"

Chapter 20

LILLY

Lilly stood outside her penthouse door. Already unlocked and ajar. She had foolishly given her wayward brother the entry code. And Tim's old key card for the sixth floor.

I'll have to amend that.

The pungent, savory scent of burning meat wafted toward her before she'd even crossed the threshold.

Lilly stopped in the kitchen doorway, crossing her arms. "What the hell do you think you're doing?"

The smell was coming from the prime broncan steak

she'd been saving to share with Brand as part of a welcome dinner for her new deputy.

Nate stood with his back to her, focusing on the pan. He flipped the steak, and the sizable piece of meat started searing, making her salivate.

He turned in a fluid motion, his rangy body belying his athleticism just as his quirky, mischievous grin masked his cleverness—not that he ever made use of either. With his narrow face, mussed brown hair, and green eyes, he was the spitting image of their deceased father while she had inherited their mother's darker looks. Just another glaring difference between them.

Nate shrugged. "I was feeling kinda peckish and I saw this lying in your fridge, so..."

"I paid half a day's salary for that."

His eyes widened. "Is it broncan?"

She huffed and stepped toward the fridge. "Don't pretend you care."

The broncan were large, domesticated mammals imported by the dworgs from their native planet. Despite their short stature, the dworgs were a hearty lot who burned through calories at double the rate of the average human—and they were particularly fond of meat. Unfortunately, though, the broncan, while common on Yerdua, had a hard time adjusting to the climate on Vox and were thus exorbitantly expensive... but pretty damn tasty.

"I'll split it with you," Nate offered.

How magnanimous. Since it's already mine.

For all his troublemaker tendencies, Nate hated being the bad guy. Lilly, however, was in no mood to assuage his guilt.

So, instead of answering, she simply shoved him away from the stove and turned off the burner.

"You can't stop cooking it in the middle," he whined. "It won't come out right."

She looked at the steak, jabbed the burner back on, and swung around to him again. "What are you doing?"

Nate frowned. "Uh, I just told you..."

"Not the meat, you ass. Yercer Taul! I mean, what the hell were you thinking?"

Nate flinched then dipped his head and examined his dusty boots, eyeballs darting to and fro under his eyelids, indicating some level of brain activity.

"You didn't *know* he was involved?"

Her brother shook his head.

"Well, maybe next time, you should find out about all the parties entangled in your dumbass scheme. *Before* agreeing to it, that is."

"Honestly, sis." Nate caught her gaze, his eyes ablaze with contrition. "I would never have done that."

"What?" she snapped. "Sold fake meds to poor, unsuspecting miners?"

He slunk back toward the table and slumped down, cradling his jaw in his thin fingers. "Seriously, I didn't think it'd go that far."

She couldn't tell if it was all an act or not.

"Where'd you get the packaging then?" she asked.

He shrugged. "Just this guy I know."

Lilly drew herself to her full height and narrowed her eyes at him. After twenty-nine years of coexistence, he should know better than to play this game with her. He should also realize she wasn't past blasting him where it would hurt if he didn't cooperate—family ties be damned.

He nodded rapidly, as if sensing her vibe. "Three months ago, with the shipment of nano-biotics, there was this small crate of empty packaging."

Lilly's lip curled.

A likely story.

"Seriously. Grenald—"

"Grenald?" she snapped.

"Yeah, he's one of the medics that bring the shipments in."

A smoky smell alerted her. She turned around, flipped the steak, and reduced the flame on the burner. It gave her time to think. "So, this Grenald... he's stealing from the Med Council?"

"No, it's just... every once in a while, a miscellaneous crate ends up on board." Nate's hand waved vaguely.

"By magic?"

He smirked. "Serendipity."

"What kind of miscellaneous crate?"

"You know, uh, supplies."

"You mean narcotics?"

A pause. "Sometimes."

She shifted her gaze out the window, unable to bear the sight of him. "Well, I hope you're prepared to do hard time in the Tyson Mines."

The mines belonged to the city of Naillik and helped to fund the local government, including the sheriff's station. Some of the miners there were voluntary, but for others, working in the mines served as punishment for breaking the law.

When she turned back, Nate's expression was wary, but ultimately untroubled.

She forced her mind and her heart into full-on professional mode. "Brother or not... I'm sheriff in this town, and if I catch you doing anything illegal, you'll spend six months in the hospital and then do hard time in the mines, just like anyone else dealing that poison to the residents of Naillik."

Nate's nervous look vanished as he began his rationalization. He was awfully good at convincing others and himself of his "near" innocence. "Listen, I don't deal with narcotics, not really. Grenald has some contact in Bane he delivers that kind of stuff to."

The first note of unease had entered her brother's voice, and it gave her a twinge of satisfaction. It was a miracle he wasn't already working in the mines.

No, not a miracle. He had her to thank for saving his ass so many times. She'd pulled him out of trouble ever since he'd arrived on Vox. Even scrupulous Tim had either looked the other way or not followed through on charges whenever he'd caught Nate embroiled in one con or another. Tim had always done that... for her.

But this time, she actually believed her brother. Not because Nate was above selling drugs, but because there would be more profit in moving the junk through Bane.

"Look at me. You ever... *ever*... pass fake meds in Naillik or in any other town again, and I am personally gonna throw you in the mines myself. Do I make myself clear?"

He nodded reluctantly.

"Now get the hell outta my place."

Nate glanced at the broncan steak, now emitting an aroma of well-cooked meat.

"Not a chance," she growled. "Out."

At least Nate was smart enough to recognize an impossible situation. He grabbed his small backpack from the table and left the kitchen without another word or a parting glance.

A few seconds later, she heard the front door open and close. Finally, she released her breath.

She plated the steak and scooped up some jumo roots that Nate had boiled. After grabbing a fork and knife, she carried her dish into the living room and sat down in a large lounge chair. This was a big hunk of steak for one woman, but it had been an exhausting day so far and she intended to wolf it all down.

"Monitor on," she ordered mid-chew.

The Vox-P News was issuing its afternoon report, which seemed eerily appropriate. A reporter was discussing the shipment of nano-biotics currently on its way to the planet. Since the citizens only received shipments every three months, and since working—and, well, living—on Vox pretty much required the meds to survive, talk of the shipment always snagged people's attention.

She took another bite of the steak, enjoying the juicy flavor and the sensation of instant energy it infused into her veins, something that her usual bland, inorganic food failed to do. She'd cook up some sand-oysters for Brand instead. Her newest deputy looked more like the invertebrate-eating type anyway.

Sated, she switched off the news and scanned her suite. She didn't really think Nate would stoop so low as to steal anything from her home, but as sheriff, she couldn't afford to make delusional, half-assed assumptions.

Noting the enviable features and furnishings around her, she sighed in resignation. There were at least two reasons that all three partners of the Red Lady had opted for a penthouse suite at the top of the building. One, to stay close to the business and, two, because they were spacious, well-appointed apartments. Unfortunately, though, hers didn't feel like home.

Then again, since Tim died, nowhere had felt like home.

Chapter 21

SHAW

"If you lose them, Zain..." Shaw warned.

She regarded her pilot. He wasn't the type to require warnings, but she needed to lash out at someone. Zain handled the piloting as well as the navigation, and he excelled at both. Hence why she'd pulled some strings in the UNSF hierarchy to get him assigned to her crew.

"I got this, Commander." Zain's pale, impassive face gave away nothing as he pummeled the controls with his spindly fingers. Competent and often emotionless, he could have been a droid in his former life.

Jibs, meanwhile, had removed his hands from his weapons station and was now staring through the front window as their ship gyrated insanely through the asteroid field. Jibs could never be accused of possessing much talent, and she certainly hadn't pulled any strings for him, but he did have a weird knack for surviving and being useful.

Usually.

"What are you doing, Jibs?" she yelled. "Keep firing at them!"

"But we're making so many turns, we could end up doubling back into one of our own missiles," Jibs quibbled.

The command blades were equipped with both missiles and plasma blasters. The missiles caused more damage, but Jibs was right: They could possibly fly back into one of their own shots, which would cause less-than-optimal results.

"Alright, only the blasters then," she said. "Just means you'll need to hit them more."

No way would she let Bechet escape this time. She wasn't just looking for his body, she wanted to see the whole *R.L. Johnson* blown to space dust, along with any lowlife stupid enough to hitch a ride with him.

Just as she'd demanded, Jibs now focused solely on the blasters, sending blue pulses of energy toward the pirate ship. It was only a matter of time. Even though Bechet was a skilled pilot, his luck was bound to run out... sooner or later. Hopefully, before she and her crew accidentally slammed their ship into an asteroid.

Her auxiliary comms screen lit up. She'd make an effort not to bash her fist through this one. Not an easy promise, though, once Captain Pike's unwelcome mug appeared.

"Commander Shaw, this is crazy! Bechet knows more about flying in these outer reaches than any other pirate."

She unleashed a cold laugh. "Just maintain pursuit, Pike. Or are you too chicken?"

His ruddy complexion darkened further. *"I'm not killing my crew for some personal vendetta you have with Remy."*

"No, you're fulfilling the contract you agreed to with Larker Max. Since you allowed Bechet to destroy the shipment of Teez, you had better, at least, complete the back end of the agreement and make sure he can't slither away from this debacle."

"Allowed him?" Pike's nostrils flared. *"We're not responsible for you and your crew's incompetence. Hell, if I hadn't contacted you, you'd have tried to pick up that body yourself. And now, you and your people would be the dead ones, not Langston and the crew of the* Kapriano.*"*

"Just do your damn job." Shaw clicked off the comms.

Sticklers like Pike bored her more than anything. What

was his problem anyway? Did the man still feel some mis-guided loyalty toward Bechet?

No, of course, not.

He was merely quivering in his boots, picturing Larker Max's reaction to the destroyed Teez. Fear drove him, as it did most people. It was the only reason the *Mearle* still flew along-side them.

She turned her focus back to her crew.

Zain was twisting the ship through tight spaces, match-ing every move the *R.L. Johnson* made. He looked quite smug about it, too. He had, no doubt, overhead Pike's "incompe-tence" remark, which had probably rankled him.

"We're not gaining?" she asked, merely to stir him up even more.

"Damn," Jibs shouted from the far side. "Almost got one of their rear starboard-side engines."

She heaved an impatient sigh. "Almost?"

They were spinning through what resembled an impos-sible barrier of rocks. With asteroids of every kind—from peb-bles to enormous masses twice the size of Earth's moon—it made for some horrific flying. She tried to read Zain's face for their chances of getting out alive, but as usual, he revealed nothing.

"Commander, I've heard rumors of several large portals somewhere in this area," Zain announced when they'd reached a somewhat clearer patch.

At first, she didn't want to answer him. It meant acknowledging that those stories were more than simple rumors. In fact, they were the bane of her existence. A few of her previous pursuits had abruptly ended with the criminals she tracked flying their vessels through such portals. Half the time, the pirate ships in question were never heard from again.

Portals were the cheater's way out of a good, honest fight, ship to ship, in one dimension. The coward's route. And very likely, the path Bechet was banking on.

Zain was still looking at her, patiently awaiting a reply even while he nudged the nav controls. His gray eyes held only the tiniest suggestion of unease.

"Yeah, OK, OK," she said testily. "There probably are portals around here somewhere. We have to keep that in mind."

Who knew what had happened to those vanishing pirates? Some had definitely had no idea what they were getting into. Others must have known where the portals would spit them back out. Since the whole Newton's Gate incident, the portals had not only changed the face of Earth but had also made policing outer space that much more difficult.

"But," she added savagely, "we're not gonna let that bastard get anywhere near those freaking portals. I swear, Zain, earn that massive pay package of yours today and close the distance, so we can blow that ship to hell."

Chapter 22

REMY

The *R.L. Johnson* wasn't too far from what Remy hoped would be their escape exit, but Shaw had gotten to be a real pain in the ass.

He had to double back and swing the *Jay* through some pretty tight spaces in order to keep ahead of her. The sharp angles of her command blade were a constant fixture in the rearview screen, as the ship swooped and lurched in mocking synchronization. She had one hell of a navigator on board, and she wasn't going to give up while Remy was still alive.

Remy steered the *Jay* toward a moon-sized rock and dove the ship through a narrow crevice. He knew the maneuver would probably drain the blood from Dreyla and Tosh's faces.

OK, maybe just Drey. Tosh probably envisioned it as an amusement ride of sorts.

Another glance at the rear-view screen told him his cool maneuver hadn't shaken his pursuers, but at least they had dropped back a bit. Shaw's pilot might've been skilled—the *Mearle*'s, too—but nobody knew this area like he did. And no one could pull off the kind of flying he was prepared to do. They were now well into the asteroid field, just where he wanted to be.

"Oh, man, if you're gonna be pulling this kind of crap, I'm gonna need another hit," Tosh said, flapping his hand at the dizzying vista of rocks blocking their path. He rose and wandered off the bridge.

So much for the amusement ride.

Remy and Dreyla exchanged a look.

"You never answered my question," she said.

"What question was that?"

"The one pertaining to whether we live or die?"

"Oh, that." Remy applied extra engine thrust, making Dreyla grab her nav console for support. "We've been through worse than this, right?"

No answer.

Remy blinked sweat from his eyes and forced a grin. "It's just like flying through a cave."

He had considerable experience with this kind of crazy-ass piloting; you just had to know how fast you could go and when exactly to turn. You also needed a sprinkling of luck on top or, at least, a lack of bad luck. And finally, you needed to keep a cool head.

Remy jerked the steering wheel hard to his left. The *Mearle* tried to follow suit but scraped one of her rear engines against a canyon wall. Shaw's ship almost collided with her fellow pursuer.

"Hah," Remy whooped. "Buh-bye, Jason."

The sight of Pike's ship hurtling away into space behind them was the second best he'd had all day. The first being the utter destruction of the *Kapriano*.

Maybe we'll get through this after all.

He soared out of the crevice and slammed forward at full throttle, but he didn't feel the power he wanted. He had lied to Shaw. The engines still weren't operating at their maximum yet. All the indicators lolled pathetically in the yellow zones.

An enormous blast rang in his ears. The *Jay* shuddered and creaked and then sank at an ugly angle toward a medium-sized asteroid. His best guess? One of their engines had been hit.

He slapped any controls that might stabilize them, but

nothing was helping. "OK, there's a chance we're gonna crash."

Dreyla's face paled, her mouth frozen in a small O shape.

He continued to make adjustments. This was his ship, after all. He knew her better than the back of his hand.

But something felt off. He hit his tablet, and the pounding guitar from Tab Benoit's "Night Train" blared across the bridge.

That's more like it.

"Hell, Captain," Dreyla mused, using the tone of a scared girl trying to be brave, "I never would've made it out of the Geddon Mines if it weren't for you."

Another way of saying she trusted him, even while petrified about their imminent demise.

As Remy well knew, slavers had captured a newborn Dreyla from a transport ship headed out to one of the mining facilities deep in the Belt. Her parents, whom she'd never really known, had likely been killed in the encounter, and she'd been tossed into the system, raised in a slave colony on Dihous Four. By the time she was eight, she was working in the mines on Kofax Prime, where Remy had ultimately rescued her.

Those were memories that Drey had tried to block out. She'd often told him that her life had begun when he saved her. And he'd often told *her* that his had as well. As far as he was concerned, they were a real family. Always and forever. And he'd do everything he could to protect her from harm.

"Captain, should I shoot up some more?" Tosh asked over the ship's comms. *"Seems like we're taking some heavy hits... thought maybe I should as well."*

Remy blinked at the console speaker in disbelief, then chuckled and leaned toward the mic. "Well, hell, Tosh, I wouldn't want it to go to waste or anything."

If the drugs kicked in right away, the old doctor might not even feel the ship exploding around him.

The *Jay*'s power flared back up, and Remy had absolute control over her once again.

"There they are," Dreyla panted.

She was pointing ahead, where a familiar light illuminated several asteroids.

A euphoric, if insane, hope swamped Remy's senses. He could discern several colors, which meant more than one portal was open. He'd only flown through a bright blue one before, the gateway that had transported him and the ship to the dark side of the moon. He had no idea where the others led and, quite frankly, didn't want to find out.

Might not get so lucky this time.

The trick, however, was that these particular portals weren't always available. Sometimes, the rifts in time and space that had occurred thanks to the Newton's Gate explosion had minds of their own. As he recalled, the blue one he now sought only opened for three-minute intervals, every half-hour. He needed to hit the location at exactly the right time and make sure Shaw was far enough behind that she couldn't easily pursue.

Once on the dark side of the moon, he could point the *Jay* in almost any direction and be far beyond Commander Shaw's reach. No way for her to track him.

Remy pushed the *Jay*'s engines as hard as possible by overriding all safety mechanisms and stealing power from life support. In the middle of such herculean efforts, his main screen lit up with Shaw's face.

"You should have given yourself up when you had the chance," came her clipped voice, just a little out of sync with her sneering, porcelain face, making her seem even more robotic than usual.

He winked at her then cut the link.

Remy looped the *Jay* around a group of small asteroids, avoiding the shots Shaw's subordinates had aimed at them even as she'd been talking. The *Jay* couldn't take much more abuse, but Remy's timing needed to be impeccable if he was going to lose the commander.

"What about the stories of some portals appearing and disappearing? Are they true as well?" Dreyla asked, her voice somewhat recovered as she jabbed at her controls.

"That would be a big affirmative. I know there are at least four portals in this area. I got lucky and happened to take the one that led somewhere... well, they all might lead somewhere, but Big Blue gets us where we want to be."

The portal he sought usually appeared near an enormous, donut-shaped asteroid that never seemed to budge from its spot. Once finding it, he might need to lose Shaw first and then double back. There were a lot of *ifs* and *maybes* in his plan, but at the moment, it was the only one he had.

He spotted the telltale ring floating ahead of them. A portal shimmered on its left side.

"That's it," he said. "Next to that big chocolate donut thing. That's our escape portal. It's now or never—"

Another blast cut him off, but he kept his hands clenched on the steering wheel. Sheer desperation and survival instincts guided his movements now. He hardly registered what his arms were doing anymore. Some weird muscle memory had kicked in, maneuvering the ship in ruthless turns between massive asteroids. Remy's whole world was reduced to the rocks and shimmering pools in front and the sliver of space that separated the *Jay* from Shaw's ship in the rear.

Unfortunately, Shaw wasn't falling behind far enough, fast enough.

In the very last second, he made a desperate run for the ever-narrowing sliver of space between two giant asteroids set to collide. The right edge of his mouth pulled up in a half-grin.

He had this. This is where he belonged. He was at one with the ship and she responded in kind.

When he was able to suck in his next breath, he knew they'd cleared it. And the command blade had been forced to pull back.

Yes!

He hit full power and guided the ship toward the desired portal.

We're gonna make it.

"Remy," Dreyla rasped, puncturing his focus, "you're bringing us in awfully fast."

His eyes didn't leave the view ahead. There were two portals in the same location, both made of glowing light. One was dark red; the other, the one he needed, bright blue.

"Shaw can't see which portal we've flown though. Gotta get there fast before they pick up our trail."

Or else we're dead anyway.

"Better buckle up," he added, snapping his own seatbelt in place.

The donut loomed ahead of them. Easily the size of a

large city.

With a coaxing whisper—"Come on, baby"—Remy urged the final push of acceleration from the *Jay*'s exhausted engines.

Just as Tab Benoit strummed his last chord, the giant blue portal blinked out. The red one vanished as well. Both were replaced by a green shimmer as a portal Remy had never seen before swallowed the *Jay* whole.

"No," Remy gasped.

And then everything turned black.

Chapter 23

SHAW

"I'm telling you," Jibs insisted, "the *Johnson* went through that portal."

Zain shook his head and turned to his superior. "I don't know, Commander. The UNSF hasn't logged any portals this far out. We have no idea where they go."

"Shaw," the comms system buzzed.

It was the *Mearle*. Apparently, the ship hadn't hit an asteroid as she figured—or at least hoped—it would.

She hit the button to respond. "Captain, I see you managed to survive."

Zain brought up a view of the *Mearle* on one of Shaw's

screens. The pirate ship was puttering along, obviously damaged but mostly intact.

"*Let me guess,*" Pike said, "*Remy went through that portal.*"

"Do you have any idea where it leads?" she asked.

"*Not really. Remy once mentioned a blue portal that shot him out on the dark side of the moon. Never said anything about a green one.*"

"So, the answer would be *no,*" she replied as she moved to cut off the transmission.

"*Shaw, we have Larker Max coming in on the broadwave,*" the captain of the *Mearle* informed her. "*He must be bouncing it off one of the mining facilities at the edge of the Belt.*"

Terrific. Just what I need.

"I'll take it," she said.

"*Commander, he wants to speak to both of—*"

But she cut the link before Pike could finish his sentence.

"Zain, block all comms to and from the *Mearle,*" she ordered.

With a curt nod, he turned back to his station.

Reluctantly, Shaw sat in her chair and pivoted toward one of the still-functioning screens. She opened the comms again, and this time, a familiar but unwelcome egg-shaped head popped onto the screen.

"Shaw, is Remy Bechet dead?" Larker demanded. *"And where is my damn shipment of Teez?"* Bits of whatever he was eating hit his camera, making her want to puke.

How did I ever get involved with this scumbag?

"Gone," she stated.

His face turned a deep purple. *"Bechet is gone?!"*

"Both are gone," she replied. "So's the *Kapriano*."

"You've really screwed this up, Shaw," he said. *"Now you owe me even more. You need—"*

"You know what, Larker, you can piss right off. I owe you nothing. You and I... we're done," she said with cold confidence.

Both Zain and Jibs gaped at her as if she'd lost her mind.

"You're done when I say you are," Larker replied, seething.

Shaw could see the pirate king signaling one of his people off camera.

"If you're trying to communicate with the Mearle, *we've blocked her comms. She'll not be firing on us anytime soon. In fact, she won't be firing on anyone, ever again."*

Larker's elongated face turned even darker, as if ready to pop.

"Boys, target the *Mearle*. Blow her to space dust."

Zain and Jibs did as they were told. A moment later, after an intense flash of light, she could see the *Mearle* floating in bits.

"You bitch," Larker spat. *"You're gonna pay for this."*

She cut the comms and turned toward her two crew members, hoping they'd continue to follow her lead. She raised her right hand and pointed her metallic forefinger at the portal.

In response, the ship powered up, and the giant green portal, the size of a huge building, grew closer. It also started to flicker, as if it didn't plan to stay long.

"Hit it!" she commanded.

The blade flew into the portal just as it was collapsing into itself.

Then, darkness engulfed the ship—and the three people on board.

Chapter 24

REMY

Remy awoke to flashing emergency lights.

OK, still alive.

The backup batteries had kicked in, but they appeared to be the only things with power. He waited for pain to kick in, too, but other than a neck strain, he was uninjured.

He searched through the semidarkness for Dreyla. Her chair was empty. His gaze shifted, and he spotted her... sprawled out against a rear electrical panel.

"Drey!" He wrenched himself free from his chair and rushed to her side in an instant. He knelt onto the floor and propped up her head and shoulders, cradling her in his arms, shaking her gently. "Drey."

Thank God, she's breathing.

"Drey," Remy urged.

An agonizing moment later, she stirred and her eyelids slowly lifted. A serene smile lit her face when she saw him. "Captain? We're OK? Wh-what happened?"

When he didn't answer, she sat up, frowning, and impatiently swiped long, curly strands of hair off her face as she scanned the bridge in rapid sweeps. Blood dripped down her forehead into the outer crease of her right eye, but she didn't seem aware of it.

"You've got a gash." With his finger, Remy indicated the spot on his own face.

It would leave a scar for sure. Well, she was a pirate. Scars came with the job description.

She flapped her hands at his concern, grasped the edge of the nearby panel, and hoisted herself up to standing, wobbling ominously.

Remy rose and put a steadying arm around her. "You need to take it easy, girl. Wait here."

He stepped quickly across the floor, flipped open a small compartment at the back of the bridge, and removed a first-aid kit. Before he could return to his injured daughter,

153

though, she appeared at his side, jostling his elbow.

"We should let Tosh handle it. You've got other things..."

"Tosh, crap..." Remy groaned. "I better make sure the old man is intact."

Just then, there came the sound of shoes clunking on the main corridor to the bridge. Tosh appeared in the doorway, a small portable light illuminating his craggy features from below, which made him seem even more ancient, almost wizard-like, than usual.

Remy sighed and leaned against the wall, relieved to see the old stoner.

"Captain, Dreyla, are you both alright?" Tosh asked.

He was in doctor mode, all traces of his dazed self gone. Remy had witnessed this uber-serious side before, even in moments when he was amazed that Tosh could stand up. *This* being one of those moments. How, after all, had the old man managed to endure the crash without obvious injury?

"Glad you could join us." Remy indicated Dreyla's face. "Can you patch her up nice and pretty?"

"I'll do my darned best." Tosh moved toward her, ignoring the first-aid kit in Remy's hands. "No pun intended."

Wincing at the corny joke, Remy watched as Tosh lifted the lantern, wiped away the blood on Drey's face, and then administered a pen-shaped medi-device to her wound.

"I still don't know what happened," Remy admitted. "We hit the portal, and everything went black."

"Ouch," Dreyla protested, shrinking back from the doctor's treatment.

"Sorry, kiddo," Tosh said. "Gotta disinfect. No time for local anesthesia." He touched the gash more gently. "How 'bout you tell us what you remember?"

"When it happened," she said, her face crinkling in concentration, "it felt like we were falling..."

"Yeah, the dampeners must've fired, but how?" Remy asked. "Without the main power, they shouldn't have."

"Oh, I managed to manually switch them to battery." She caught his gaze and beamed with pride.

Aha.

That was why she'd gotten out of her seat. The move had nearly cost Drey her life. But it had also saved all of theirs.

"Well, of all the crazy-ass ideas..." he said, "that one takes the prize."

Her grin widened.

He couldn't help grinning back. The girl was insane but also a genius. While the ship's dampeners usually required more power, the battery banks must've had just enough juice to stop the *Jay* from going *splat* on the planet... whichever planet they'd landed on.

His gaze shifted toward the front windows, at the arid landscape outside.

"Where do you s'pose we are?" Dreyla asked, as if reading Remy's mind. Again.

"Not sure," he replied.

"Beats me." Tosh finished sealing the gash on Drey's forehead.

As usual, his handiwork impressed Remy. Perhaps she wouldn't have a noticeable scar after all.

Free again, Dreyla immediately darted to the bow to look out the ship's windows.

"The portal changed," Remy mused. "From the blue one that would've taken us to the dark side of the moon."

"Changed to what?" Dreyla asked.

"Green... that's pretty much the extent of my knowledge," Remy lamented. "I've never seen that portal before, and quite frankly, I have no freakin' clue where it dumped us out."

Remy joined her at the transparent steel windows. He remained standing and said nothing, just absorbing the vista outside.

"Is this Earth?" Dreyla asked.

There were portals that lead from Earth to various locations in outer space, and vice versa. The terrain before them resembled a desert, not unlike the ones in southern Arizona that Remy had hiked through in his youth.

"Maybe we landed somewhere in the Southwest," he ventured.

"Southwest?" Dreyla asked.

"Of the United States."

"I don't think so," Tosh said, the glazed look once again overcoming him. "Never seen the moon that close."

Indeed, a large looming object hung in the rosy-orange sky above. An enormous and much-too-close moon. If Earth's moon had ever gotten that close, it would've wreaked havoc on the planet.

"We definitely aren't in Kansas anymore," Remy quipped.

Dreyla rolled her eyes.

Remy had never been to Kansas, but he still found the saying strangely comforting. As with all obscure cultural references, Dreyla disliked it, mainly because it made no sense to her. Which made it even more amusing to him.

"Right. I think we can safely rule out Earth," he said. "On account of the giant moon and all. But we know they've discovered portals that lead to other planets."

While the blue portal he'd used before was based in their solar system, there were in fact portals all over the planet and some on the moon. Hell, he'd heard reports of them being discovered on Mars, on other moons, and even on some of the larger asteroids. Supposedly, many of those gateways led to planets in other galaxies or universes.

It was clear the portal they'd flown through had taken them somewhere alien to them. With any luck, somewhere in their galaxy, or at least somewhere in their universe. He wasn't confident his monkey brain could handle anything more foreign than that.

Remy turned his attention to the task of bringing the power back up. But tweaking, rebooting, and, in a temper, finally kicking the control unit all produced nothing.

He avoided eye contact with his two shipmates. Not knowing which universe they were stuck in made him feel off-kilter and far less captain-like than he cared to admit. He just had to trust that answers would present themselves eventually. Because, for now, there were more pressing issues... like why they had no power.

"Right, we need to assess the damage," he said, straightening. "Drey, head down to the engine room. See if you can figure out what's up with the power. If the *Jay*'s just broken, let's get her fixed."

"On it." Dreyla trotted off the bridge, clearly relieved to be doing something.

He turned to Tosh. "In case we don't get the good old hospitality of Earth out there, we'll need enviro suits. Maybe a scanner, too."

Tosh nodded.

"And Tosh," Remy said before the doctor could get far, "I don't think we need the bulkier suits. The lightweight ones should do."

"What are you going to do, Captain?" Tosh's voice

sagged with trepidation. Not even the drugs could mask that.

Remy's main job now was to appear to be on top of things so that neither Tosh nor Drey flew into a total panic. Intergalactic culture shock tended to have that effect on people, even when you knew where you'd landed. This interstellar mystery tour wasn't for the faint of heart.

He flashed the old man a confident smile. "I'm gonna see if I can link my personal tablet to the batteries and then MacGyver 'em both to the array on top of the *Jay*... see if I can't get a fix on where we are."

It all seemed too much for the old man, even though he likely got Remy's ancient television reference. Nodding vaguely, he turned and shuffled off.

Remy rummaged through all the cabinets on the bridge, amassing a stash of wires and tools. He then proceeded to link his tablet to an emergency-light line below his console. The elecronic device had its own power source but would gobble through that in seconds with the applications he needed to run.

He then had to link the navigational array to the battery lines, which required busting open a panel under Drey's console. He wasn't even sure if the array could run off batteries. It was definitely a huge power suck, so his location search would have to be quick or they'd end up wandering through the ship in the dark. This unintended excursion was bad enough without that happening.

He secured the connection, returned to his station, and

started the scan app, a slimmed-down version of the ship's native navigational software. It flickered to life.

Bingo.

A small, barely decipherable star map appeared on his tablet. The app was running pattern-recognition algorithms on the data the array had picked up. So far, it recognized nothing. Then, the line under Drey's console sparked and caught fire.

"Crap," he snarled at the flames.

He leapt from his chair, bounded across the bridge, yanked an extinguisher from an alcove, and blasted the fire out in a few seconds, leaving a puffy ball of foam beneath Drey's station.

Well, that worked great.

Small mercies, it hadn't blown his tablet. Since it contained all his music, that would've been a major bummer, even if Drey might beg to disagree. What was he supposed to annoy her with if he didn't have his blues? Half the joy of living would be gone.

A little flashing message drew his focus back to the app. The scan had finished. He pulled the screen closer to discover the name of their current solar system.

But the screen had only a brief message for him in faint, almost apologetic, letters:

<Scan inconclusive>

Remy sank into his chair, forehead in his hands. What else could he do?

Chapter 25

LILLY

Lilly sat at her desk, flicking through various listings of local disturbances on her tablet. Which scum of the universe would she tackle first? And would it be before she took her dinner break, or after?

Not that she was all that hungry following her enormous mid-afternoon snack.

With a weary sigh, she skimmed another police report. Brad Raymar was complaining—again—that kids had broken into the food stores down at his mining camp. A legitimate beef perhaps, but Lilly found herself wishing he'd simply improve his security measures and stop bugging her about it.

Emiline Ler, meanwhile, had filed an assault charge against two new miners, a James Teman and an Alan Fiennes. Both men had been questioned and released, but they had since decided to file charges of their own. Emiline had a history of shakedown cons, offering her services as a prostitute, refusing to service the clients, and then finally claiming assault if the men didn't pay her what she wanted. Was it time for the scam artist to taste her own poison?

Lilly flicked to the next complaint. Before she'd even read the summary, though, the comms in her office buzzed.

"Sheriff, Mayor Cansen is here to see you," came Pierce's soft-spoken voice.

Without waiting for a response, Mayor Jett Cansen crashed through her door. Clearly frazzled, he wiped his sweaty brow with a square cloth. His brown suit nearly burst at the seams, and his round face was flushed from either exertion or alarm—Lilly wasn't sure which.

The guy had a serious blood-pressure issue that no number of local meds seemed able to fix. Being the mayor of Naillik was certainly stressful, but the sheer volume of fried sand-oysters the man ate couldn't be helping his situation.

"We got a problem," Cansen announced, panting slightly.

"We've got many problems, Mayor Cansen." Lilly waved at her tablet and rose from her desk.

Cansen never—ever—sat down in her office, and she

didn't want to look up at him from her chair.

"We just got word that Med Ship Vox 2 landed an hour ago," Cansen continued.

"But... they weren't due for another two days."

Lilly consulted her display for the date on her calendar. She was pretty sure about this.

Yes, correct.

She enlarged the calendar for Cansen's benefit.

"Well, they didn't get the memo," he said gruffly. "Cuz it's already here."

Admittedly, she didn't understand the emergency. So, the nano-biotics that Voxians required to survive had arrived earlier than expected... wasn't that a positive thing?

"Forgive me for being obtuse, but what's the problem? Something go wrong at the landing port?"

Cansen sighed melodramatically, as if fed up with a confused toddler. "You don't get it. The ship landed somewhere in the desert."

"Wait, what?" Lilly fingered her temple and strode to the window. "OK, OK, let me think." With her back to the mayor, she stared out at nothing in particular. "We get a team over there pronto to pick up Naillik's share of the meds. And then get the rest to their proper distribution centers."

When she turned to him again, Mayor Cansen's face had

screwed up, causing droplets of sweat to trickle over his cheeks.

"We can't raise them on comms. There's been no communication beyond the notification they sent out when they broke through atmo."

Lilly absorbed the situation in silence, then said, "This is... not good."

He patted his forehead again. "If we don't get that shipment of nano-biotics, thousands of..."

He didn't need to finish the thought. She nodded gloomily.

"Those with the Rot won't make it long enough for the next shipment," he added, pacing in a circle, wringing his hands. "And we're talking about more than a few citizens."

That was her immediate concern. One of her main duties, after all, was making sure the citizens of Naillik received their necessary meds on time. She couldn't fulfill that responsibility if the shipment had been hijacked—or destroyed—and she wouldn't let herself ruminate on the fact that the quarterly supply was intended for the entire planet.

A disturbing thought abruptly popped into her brain. What were the odds that an anonymous source would tip her off about Yercer's shady dealings on the same day that the eagerly awaited med ship would crash in the desert? Was it a mere coincidence that the vitally important shipment of nans had arrived two days earlier than expected?

Lilly sighed forlornly. She didn't believe in coincidences... not when Gono Darkbur was likely involved.

She hit her comms and switched to the global setting so that every deputy would hear. "We have a *code one* emergency. I repeat, *code one*. Everyone needs to gather in the staff room in ten minutes."

She switched over to a different channel. "Skully?"

Nothing.

Lilly avoided eye contact with the mayor as she repeated the call. "Skul-ly!"

Another excruciatingly long moment passed.

Dammit, where is he?

Not the best time, after all, for Naillik's number-one mechanic and owner of the shipyard to be on break.

"*Sheriff?*" Skully replied at last.

"I need the department's drop ship on top of the building in fifteen," she barked.

"*But, Sheriff, I still need a couple more days with her. You see, the rear intake valves are—*"

"Fifteen minutes, Skully, or people die. Lots of them."

"*On my way,*" he replied hurriedly.

Chapter 26

REMY

Going through the strange portal had warped Remy's sense of time, but it seemed as if a whole hour had passed before Tosh reported back to the bridge. Luckily, though, he bore three lightweight enviro suits, as ordered. Remy decided to forgo asking the stoned doc what had taken him so long.

After handing Remy two of the suits, Tosh attempted to don the third, which proved to be a difficult task. He spent several minutes fumbling with the safety clasps on the suit's torso. When he finally got it open and stepped into the legs, he wavered on one foot as if about to topple over but then righted himself at the last second.

This seemed like a man who'd never worn such a suit before.

Is that even possible? Come to think of it... maybe it is.

He and Tosh had spent more than fifteen years together on the *R.L. Johnson*, but in all that time, the doc had never stepped foot off the ship if she wasn't safely docked. He'd never been part of a boarding party when they'd taken other ships by force, nor had he ever ventured outside on any of the asteroids where the crew had pulled a slew of perilous jobs. As the ship's sole medic, he was too valuable to risk—even when Remy could've used an extra set of hands.

No wonder Tosh looked as though he were fighting with an octopus.

"Haven't you ever worn one of those?" Drey asked, stepping onto the bridge.

Tosh stalled his battle. "Nope, and for darn good reason."

"Not even on Mars?" Dreyla approached Tosh, eyeing him curiously.

"Never been outside any of the bases there. I leave hostile environments to the masochists."

"Here." Smiling, she helped him shove his arm into one of the sleeves.

"When you're finished playing maid, Drey, can you fix

our power, please?" Remy rose from his chair, still clutching the two enviro suits. "We only got battery juice and it's kinda cramping my style."

Drey looked at him darkly. "Something's not right. The power converters aren't getting any energy. I don't know, Captain... it's like the Teez isn't reacting with the dark matter."

"Well, why the hell not?" he demanded.

"I-I can't explain it." Turning toward her station, she spotted the foamy mess beneath the console. "What the heck happened here?"

"Uh, yeah, about that..." Remy said, rubbing his jaw. "I was trying to figure out where we landed. Long story short, I still don't have a clue." He handed Drey one of the enviro suits. "So, first, we should assess the damage and then solve our little power problem."

Remy unfastened the suit and slipped it over his clothes. Dreyla copied him. They clicked their belts shut at the same time.

Tosh stared at them. "How'd you...?" he asked in an awed voice, as if he'd never seen them suit up before. "Oh, never mind." He continued to fumble with his own fasteners.

Remy secured his helmet and then cocked his head toward the exit. "Let's have a look around, shall we?"

He gave Tosh another minute to finish securing his protective gear and then led his two crewmates through the ship, to the starboard-side airlock in the cargo hold. Unfortunately, the port-side one had sustained too much damage in the fire-fight.

The three of them walked into the airlock, manually closed the door behind them, and opened the outer door. Stepping out of the ship presented no problems as the *Jay* had sunk down in the sand and presently sat about a foot above the ground.

Remy and Dreyla trekked around the perimeter of the ship to survey the damage from the space battle as well as the rough landing. Besides the trashed port-side airlock, many panels had flown off, and only one of the rear blasters was still intact. A massive gash and several charred holes marred the cargo hold's outer walls, and some of the armor along both sides of the vessel had crumpled. Worse, at least one of their engines seemed in need of extensive repair.

"Poor baby," Dreyla murmured, smoothing her gloved hand along the ship's exterior.

"She's seen worse," Remy said. "She'll live to see more."

Dreyla stared at a large deflector array that dangled from the ship. Since it provided protection from everything, ranging from plasma blasts to small asteroid hits, it was a fairly critical feature.

"That ain't gonna be cheap," Dreyla said with a sigh. "Someone's gonna have to sell an organ or two."

"Yeah, but we got a bigger problem," Remy growled. "Straight ahead."

She swung around to follow his gaze. A large, six-legged creature lumbered toward Tosh, who was utterly oblivious, preoccupied with being Tosh.

"What the hell is that?!" Dreyla screamed. "TOSH!"

Remy sped toward the doc, raising his pistol.

The blasts jolted Tosh out of his trance. He spun around, looking totally lost until he spotted the oncoming creature. Remy managed to sink half a dozen shots into the beast, which slid in the sand and came to rest at the doctor's feet.

"Whoa, guess that was a close call?" Tosh panted, staring down at the creature.

Remy had made his last shot from only three meters away, landing it right between the eyes. That was the kill shot—and a good thing for Tosh.

The creature resembled a mixture of cow, tiger, and lizard, but its mouth had layers of fangs, and its mane comprised spiky, leather-like flaps of skin. The beast had moved via its four rear legs. Upon closer inspection, it seemed the front two were meant solely for shredding its prey.

"Hmm, interesting," Tosh said. "A hexapod. Or perhaps, more accurately, a quadruped. Mammalian or reptilian—hard to determine." He poked its leathery skin. Prodded its muscles. "Young, I'm guessing." Then he pulled back the rubbery lips to examine its orange-tinted teeth and fangs.

When he bent closer to check its nether regions, Remy cleared his throat.

The doctor glanced up at him. "Hermaphrodite, both male and female."

"To me, it's an it," Remy said. "A dead it. Can you just leave the thing—"

Abruptly sensing trouble, he shifted his gaze to the horizon and looked down into a spacious valley of boulders and sand dunes. After a few seconds, he stiffened.

"What?" Tosh asked.

"We're not alone."

The doctor chuckled. "Well, of course not. This creature…" He frowned, finally catching his captain's meaning.

Remy used his helmet's magnifier to zoom in on a shiny object some five miles away. Yep, it was a ship, or a craft of some kind. He didn't recognize the make, but it was quite a bit smaller than the *Jay*.

"What kind of ship is that?" Dreyla asked, stepping up to them.

"Beats me."

It felt weird for Remy to admit that. He thought he knew every type of vessel ever made. Again, this did not bode well for determining where the portal might've taken them.

While Remy and Drey fixated on the mysterious spacecraft, Tosh proceeded to shut out the world again, still fascinated by the giant beast.

Remy sighed. "We'd better load up on weapons. Between whatever the hell that thing is…" He pointed at the dead creature. "...and whoever's on that ship..."

"You never know when you might need a good blaster," Dreyla said, finishing her father's thought.

They both watched as Tosh flipped up the front plate of his helmet.

"Holy crap, Tosh!" Remy yelled, bounding toward the doctor.

Tosh stalled him with an outstretched palm. "It's OK, Cap. I used the suit's diagnostics, plus the scanner, to determine atmosphere. It's similar to Earth's." He flashed his slightly manic grin.

Remy flipped up his own shield and took a tentative breath, then a deeper one. The air smelled like the American Southwest... and burned with the dry heat of that region. And for a delicious moment, he could nearly let himself believe that was where they'd crash-landed... except for the little matter of that giant moon in the sky.

Now that his eyes had fully adjusted to the muted light outside the ship, he also noticed that the sky itself was different. Half of it, near the humongous moon, had a blue tinge, similar to Earth's, while the other half was more greenish in color, and the rosy orange of sunset melded with both.

He wiped his brow clear of the sweat that had almost instantly formed.

Tosh consulted his atmo-gauge. "Yeah, it's thirty-two point two degrees Celsius—or ninety degrees Fahrenheit if you're old school."

"Pretty toasty," Remy said, following Dreyla back inside the ship for a few extra weapons.

"No kidding," she grumbled. "If it's this hot near sunset, wonder what it's like at midday?"

Remy didn't answer. He was too busy ruminating on the doc's "old school" comment, which, to be fair, described just about everything he did.

His odd ways often mystified his crewmates, especially Dreyla. Not Tosh, though—the old doc had at least fifty years on him, if not more. He'd existed well before the whole Newton's Gate incident had changed Earth and her solar system forever.

As innovative as Tosh could be from a medical standpoint, he definitely had old-fashioned tendencies of his own. Back when they'd first met, he'd even told Remy about his extensive collection of antique vinyl albums, many featuring the kind of music his would-be captain liked. That little revelation had certainly influenced Remy's willingness to hire Tosh onto the *Jay*'s crew, a decision that had ultimately paid off in dividends. Tosh, after all, was a master doctor—and a reliable, kindhearted guy—once you got past his many quirks.

"OK, guys," Remy said as he and Drey returned from their weapon-gathering mission, "time to move out. We're losing light, and it's a long walk to that other ship." He checked his ammo, then stuffed his Colt into a side holster.

"Should we take off our suits?" Dreyla asked. "Easier to tromp through the sand without them."

He shook his head, then tugged his helmet back on. "We need to keep the suits, or we'll fry out here."

At least their battery packs would last longer without having to supply oxygen. Maybe this streak of good luck would continue when they encountered the owners of that ship.

After donning her own helmet, Dreyla shut the airlock's outer door, readjusted the four blades sheathed at various places on her body, and took up her plasma rifle as if she meant business. Remy nodded approvingly at her badass appearance.

When he shifted his attention to Tosh, Remy's admiration turned to annoyance. The doc was still prodding the beast, muttering classification details to himself.

"Tosh, forget that lump of meat," Remy said. "Chances are, whatever's on that ship is gonna be a helluva lot more fascinating."

Chapter 27

LILLY

"Mayor," Lilly said, holstering her pistols, "we don't have time to question him right now, but I have the feeling that Yercer Taul might have some answers for us."

"Taul? You have *Taul* in custody?" Cansen's head twisted instinctively in the direction of the door leading to the holding cells.

She grinned. "Oh, you hadn't heard? He's sitting tight in A-15."

Cansen's frown deepened and his meaty forehead crinkled. "Then he can't be responsible. The man's got the perfect alibi. You."

"Yeah, I was thinking it was more likely his boss."

Letting that theory sink in, she brushed past him toward her office door. Out in the hall, she narrowly avoided colliding with Brand, who was carrying a massive MZ-99 rifle that looked way too big for her slender frame. The blaster had enough power to penetrate a concrete wall, but its bulkiness made it impractical in most situations. Though Brand's apparent strength impressed Lilly, the sheriff couldn't help but recall her deputy's previous—and rather disastrous—escapade with hefty weaponry.

"Really?" Lilly asked, scanning her deputy's uniform for any other deadly accessories.

"Uh, you said *code one*." Brand balanced the blaster in one hand as if to demonstrate its portability. Her perfectly sculpted brows hiked up. "Can't hurt."

In the short time Lilly had known her, she'd noticed Brand always favored the heavy-duty guns, most of which nobody in the department had ever used. She also enjoyed playing with the station's explosives.

Lilly reflected that maybe she should have another look at her newest deputy's psych eval.

"I can leave it on the drop ship if I have to," Brand said, her eyes downcast.

"Oh, fine, bring it," Lilly snapped.

They entered the staff room, where everyone appeared to be ready—a gratifying sight. Each officer wore his or her full uniform and was armed to the hilt, albeit with less showy weapons than Brand preferred.

Lilly didn't intend to take all of her deputies to the med ship, but she wanted those remaining behind to be prepared for trouble. Especially since she suspected a larger conspiracy at work.

"Sheriff, what's going on?" Davis asked, sliding in beside Brand in a way that smacked of shared intimacy.

Not an ideal situation perhaps, but Lilly had learned to choose her battles.

All eyes were glued on her now. This would be her biggest test since she'd accepted the job. She felt personally responsible for the shipment of drugs, just as she felt responsible for the safety of these deputies standing before her. It wouldn't be "a walk in the park"—as Tim used to say before every perilous mission.

Oh, Tim.

She missed him so much now. Was he in some mysterious dimension, gazing down on this scene, yelling words of advice she couldn't hear? Nah, she didn't believe in an afterlife. Just her mind reaching out for a crutch in a time of need.

"Somebody might be jacking our med shipment," she began. She took wide strides in front of the small crowd of a dozen officers, hoping to project calm reassurance.

"But that's not due in today," Davis pointed out.

She acknowledged him with a wry smile. "Ah, yes. Apparently, the Vox Council moved the shipment up without remembering to tell us."

As expected, a ripple of shock washed over her audience. Heads shook. People whispered to each other. Most of them had family and friends who were afflicted with the devastating disease.

"Who the hell would try to swipe the meds?" Potter's voice rang out over the murmurs, tight with fury. "Over half the people on this planet need those to survive the month, and the rest of us—" He stopped himself, the answer likely dawning on him.

"Darkbur?" Davis suggested.

Lilly shrugged, which caused another wave of speculative glances. Their sense of rage was palpable.

Good.

They'd need that fury to drive them through what lay ahead.

The comms link crackled loud enough to get everyone's attention.

"I'm on the roof," Skully announced.

That was fast. Then again, for all his impudence, he was the best ship mechanic on the planet, so his promptness shouldn't surprise her.

"OK, gang, half of you will stay here to hold down the fort," she commanded, pointing at six of her deputies. "The rest, load up and look sharp. We got a job to do."

Chapter 28

DREYLA

Dreyla laughed. "What an idiot."

Based on the helmet-cam video she and Tosh were watching, Remy had just face-planted into a small sand dune. The image had gone still, divided into two blocks of color: half golden sand, half kaleidoscopic sky.

Tosh chuckled. "And he bugs *me* about being stoned."

"Exactly." Dreyla shifted her position on the flat boulder the two of them were sharing and took a drink of water from her suit's hydration system.

She and Tosh were waiting for Remy to return from his scouting mission. He'd left the two of them here once they'd gotten within eyesight range of the strange ship.

Since the mutiny, the recent space battle, and their

crash-landing on this unknown world, Remy had become even more paternal towards her. He'd often switch to this mode whenever he sensed "real" danger.

You know, as opposed to our usual peril.

Dreyla appreciated his concern, but still, she had to put the old man in his place once in a while, to keep him humble.

Isn't that what teen daughters are supposed to do?

When he'd announced he wanted her to stay with Tosh, she'd told him to piss off. He'd then tried playing the captain card, and when that hadn't worked, he'd admitted he was concerned about the doctor's well-being—given his inexperience with off-ship excursions.

At that point, she'd surrendered. He hadn't offered her much of a choice. The hike to the ship, across an undulating desert, had been pretty exhausting, and Tosh wasn't a young man. She often worried about him, too. But she'd only agreed to stay behind on the condition that Remy would live-stream his video feed so they could see what was going on.

Hence the sitting on a giant rock, staring into a tiny screen, getting thirstier and giddier with each passing moment.

"For your amusement, I just sank up to my knees in

sand," Remy said over the comms.

So, that's why he face-planted. Pathetic.

"Are you... alright, Captain?" Tosh inquired, his lips quivering with the effort of stifling his laughter.

"Still recovering my dignity." He panted. *"But other than that, I'm fine."*

Dreyla giggled. "Oh, Captain, you lost that a long time ago."

As Remy struggled to right himself, the camera image bounced all over the place.

"Hold the camera still," she instructed, "so we can actually see something. You're giving us motion sickness here."

Remy straightened the helmet-cam and refocused, offering them a clear view of the ship. Although it had gleamed like a mint-condition craft from afar, it looked fairly weathered up close and wasn't even a quarter of the *Jay's* size. On the other hand, it seemed to have dark-matter engines—or some bizarre version of them.

Dreyla sat up, peering closer. "Captain, zoom in on those rear engines so I can get a better look."

"You bet."

She studied the enlarged image, tracing the contours with her gloved fingers.

"What are you thinking?" Remy asked.

"Weird," Dreyla mused. "They look like the engines did when they were first invented."

"Do you want me to kick the tires while I'm at it?" Remy asked, zooming back out.

Tosh snorted.

Yet another of their inside jokes that she didn't get—and didn't feel like asking to have explained to her right now. She opened her mouth to change the subject when the words froze in her throat. Half a dozen figures bolted out of the ship. And they were unmistakably human.

She clutched Tosh's forearm. Remy was still crawling out of the sand, so he hadn't been spotted. But before she could ask if he'd seen *them*, his camera went still, showing the scene from a position closer to the ground. He'd either found a hidey-hole or flattened himself behind a dune. She released a ragged sigh of relief.

But even with Remy's view trained on the ship, not the fleeing figures, the image still lingered in Dreyla's brain. Though not uniformed men, all were sturdy, muscular individuals she wouldn't want to get on the wrong side of.

While trekking toward the other ship, wondering who they might find inside, she'd expected to spy passengers of a more alien variety—especially after their encounter with that six-legged monster thing. But the men had looked decidedly human to her.

"You see if they were armed?" Remy asked, his voice

muffled.

"Yep," she replied. "Afraid so."

"And they were all human. Or human-looking at least," Tosh added. "Damn, why didn't we enable your recorder? I'd love to see them again."

Remy zoomed in on the shot Drey and Tosh were watching on the monitor. No more movement—just a stationary ship, wind-whipped sand, and multihued sky. At the sound of distant engines, the captain's helmet-cam panned in the direction of the fleeing men, but several sizable dunes blocked the view. A brewing sandstorm didn't help either.

Where the hell did they go?

As if echoing her thought, Remy whispered, *"I... don't... like this."*

"Hold on, Captain, we're heading your way." Dreyla clicked the video screen into its secure slot on the arm of her suit.

"We are?" Tosh asked, making no effort to shift his position on the large rock.

"You aren't," came Remy's voice.

Tosh smiled smugly and folded his arms. His gray eyes held a challenge.

Two against one, but she didn't care. The odds were six against one where Remy presently crouched. Besides, there was no way she'd miss boarding an alien craft. The figures, after all, counted as extraterrestrial even if they resembled humanoids.

"Come on." She grabbed Tosh by the arm and hoisted him up.

"Where are we going?" he asked.

"To the captain. And don't tell me you're not interested in exploring that ship. Or examining alien creatures."

Tosh shrugged mildly. Scientific curiosity would always win out with him.

"Now hang on a minute—" Remy snapped.

"You always taught me," she countered quickly, "that you should never go anywhere without having someone watch your back, right?"

Without waiting for a reply, she readied her blaster and began trudging through the sand in a beeline toward her captain.

Tosh trailed behind, unholstering his own weapon.

A few seconds later, Remy's unamused voice crackled through the speaker. *"Huh, so now you listen to me?"*

Chapter 29

LILLY

"Sheriff," Skully announced from the cockpit, "touch-down in less than ten minutes."

The drop ship shuddered as it hit a cloud of sand. Violet forks of lightning surged through the cloud and sizzled the front windshield. Lilly jerked back in her seat. The ship had been designed to fly through most environments, but a dose of a billion volts at close range never calmed the nerves.

"Everyone, get ready," she instructed.

She scanned her deputies, half of whom returned her gaze with determined smiles and shining irises. The other half looked terrified, their eyes avoiding hers, darting instead to the fireworks outside the windows.

Like humanity in general, her crew divided into the risk-takers and the risk-averse. It had nothing to do with skill or experience. Just inner programming. It frustrated her at times, but over the past year, she'd strived to cater to both personality types.

"We have no idea what we're about to find, but we need to be ready for a fight," she said in firm but gentle tones.

Skully, who didn't technically work for the sheriff's station but still serviced all of its vehicles, skillfully took the ship down to two thousand feet. He might not be an official employee, but he treated everyone in the department as if they were one of his own children, so even when not asked to do so, he'd often volunteer for tricky jobs like the one he was about to perform.

Flying anything around Vox's volatile skies could be difficult. If Lilly and her deputies needed to land quickly, to maintain an element of surprise, they required the drop ship—a vehicle meant for delivering troops via vertical plunge, from as high as thirty thousand feet. Frankly, though, Lilly hoped she'd never experience a descent from such a height.

The last couple thousand feet were always the toughest. All could go smoothly, of course: The pilot could just sync the thrusters to the internal pressurizers, which would keep the passengers from squishing into the ship's metal decking. But if one of Vox's sand squalls happened to blow through, the ship could find itself off course and smash into the planet's surface. It wouldn't be the first time in history. Skill alone wasn't enough; you needed luck on your side, too.

The crapstorm outside didn't bode well for their chances. Then again, very little on Vox ever did.

Was that true? Or was Lilly just stuck in a self-sabotaging *get-off-this-planet* mode? If she were honest with herself, she'd admit to being stuck in such a rut ever since her husband was killed.

"Sheriff?" Deputy Joyce's voice crackled over the comms.

He was one of the members of her staff she'd left back at the station. Like Brand, he was a newbie to the job, but unlike her, he didn't know his ass from his elbow. He was likable enough, but having him on this drop would have endangered his life and everyone else's. Not that he had begged to join the mission or anything.

Joyce had been one of the mayor's hires intended to bolster the department's numbers. A distant relative. Maybe someday he'd become a decent officer. But today was not that day.

"Yeah, what is it, Joyce?" Lilly snapped.

"The prisoners are demanding to be fed. Again."

The ship shook violently, slamming everyone against one another, and Lilly against the side panel.

"Sorry, guys!" Skully called out cheerfully.

Lilly rubbed the spot on her shoulder that had whacked against a protruding ridge on the panel. She'd have a nice bruise there later to add to her collection.

"We need to land now," Skully called over his shoulder in a more serious tone. "I see two high-altitude squalls near the med ship. Better to land here where we've got some visibility and then hike the quarter-mile in."

"Agreed," she said. "Do it."

An instant later, he started the drop.

"Sheriff, what should I do?" Joyce's voice whined.

The ship shuddered as it plunged into near free fall. Lilly grasped a side handle for support and felt her stomach bouncing upward. Nothing could ever prepare a body for such abuse, even a healthy one like hers. It was horrendous every time.

"Dammit, Joyce... use your imagination."

She cut off the comms. She honestly didn't care if Joyce chose to starve Yercer and his cohorts, as long as he didn't let them escape. Hopefully, using his imagination wouldn't result in such a scenario.

Focus, Lilly.

She needed to concentrate on the immediate mission, not on what was happening back at the station.

"I think I'm gonna be sick," Davis moaned beside her.

She threw him a sideways look of warning.

"I had half a bowl of D-Downder's stew before we left," Davis acknowledged. "I dunno... sometimes, you just want... you know, a simple b-bowl of food, where every spoonful's the same... that you can eat when you're f-focusing on something else and—"

"Shut up, Davis," she commanded.

Brand, on his other side, flashed him a sympathetic look.

The ship quaked even more violently.

Harvey Downder's stew was suspect even if you weren't dropping out of the sky. The staff of his little cafe, which lay around the corner from the sheriff's station, had a habit of cooking whatever Downder had killed or found dead around town. Protein was protein, but still, nobody ever knew how old the meat was, and for his infamous stew, the man simply covered up the gamey taste with what Lilly had to admit was an incredible blend of spices.

Still, anytime she'd eaten it, she'd made damn sure to inspect every spoonful before it went anywhere near her mouth.

The ship shook again and Davis turned a more persuasive shade of green. A moment later, he blew chunks all over Brand's boots and her big-ass weapon. Definitely not the smoothest way to woo his new conquest.

Brand glared at the hapless Davis, her thick eyelashes

descending as she narrowed her pretty eyes.

"Well... lucky it was only half a bowl," Lilly mused.

The ship slammed down to the ground. Even with the pressurizers on full, Lilly's body rattled, and the air was punched from her lungs. She felt the intense discomfort of being a delicate sack of bones, completely at the mercy of incredible forces. Laughable to think she had any control over her destiny.

All her deputies were silent now, their faces creased with anxiety and, in some cases, the euphoria of survival. Davis wasn't the only one who'd vomited. Already, the smell of puke had overwhelmed that of fuel and burnt rubber.

"Good job, Skully," Lilly croaked.

She swallowed, her throat scratchy and parched, and fumbled with the safety-belt buckle. No matter how queasy and weak she felt, she had to step up, to rouse her deputies into action and catch the bad guys. Her feelings weren't important. Neither was her sense of being abandoned by Tim. Nor her growing hatred for the planet.

Retrieving the medication, especially for all citizens suffering from the Rot, was the only thing that mattered.

Chapter 30

REMY

Remy waited for Dreyla and Tosh to reach his location. He'd removed his helmet but, as a safety precaution, remained in a crouching position behind a small sand dune, where he could observe the strange ship without being detected.

He wished the pair of them had just stayed where they were until he could ensure the coast was clear. But Drey's stubborn streak was often more resilient than he cared to admit.

Huh. Wonder where she gets that from?

"Captain, what do you think's going on?" Tosh asked, unceremoniously collapsing on the sand beside him.

Dreyla took the more graceful approach, hunkering down on one knee, removing her own helmet, and peering over the crest of the dune at the mysterious craft, gun poised.

Remy rose wordlessly and pushed ahead over the dune, pistol raised.

"Remy?" Dreyla called after him. "You OK?"

But Remy was too focused on his surroundings to respond.

The side ramp leading into the ship was down. The men had left so hastily they hadn't bothered to secure it. A variety of odd tracks led away from the craft—not just footprints, but deep depressions, as if someone had dragged several hefty crates through the sand. But the armed strangers had yet to return, and the only sound was the wind as it whipped across the desert, pelting Remy, his crewmates, and the ship with coarse particles of sand.

Remy halted at the bottom of the ramp, sheltering his eyes from the flying grit. "Here's what's gonna happen. I'm going in, and you two are staying out here."

Like any good crew, Drey and Tosh ignored his instructions and proceeded to follow him into the ship.

The sudden cold darkness came as a relief to Remy, whose eyes itched from the bright sunlight and windblown sand. But a wave of revulsion quickly followed.

Dreyla's eyes widened. "Holy crap!"

Three bodies, all appearing to be human males, lay

sprawled out on the floor of the small cargo hold. They had been riddled with gigantic blast holes, which had caused several large pools of blood to ooze onto the floor.

"Whatever these guys were hauling, someone reckoned it was valuable enough to kill them for." Remy used his foot to nudge the outstretched arm of one of the victims back toward his torso.

No doubt the gun-toting men they'd spotted were the murderers.

Merciless bastards.

Some things never changed, no matter how far you ventured into the universe.

Over half of the crews Larker Max had working for him were willing to snuff out anyone who got between them and their score. Of course, according to Captain Pike, Larker apparently feared that more pirates had come to prefer Remy's philosophy: kill only if you had to. Certainly a less messy way to go.

Remy turned toward the open doorway. Whoever had murdered these men—perhaps the figures they'd seen, perhaps not—was still out there... somewhere. He only hoped the killers had no plans to return. For this ship... or his.

Voicing similar thoughts, Dreyla said, "Can't believe they didn't hear us crash or spot the *Jay*, but I'm too grateful to question it."

"You and me both," Remy muttered.

Turning back to the three victims, he realized none of them were armed—although, in theory, any weapons they'd possessed could've been removed after death. The only accessory they appeared to have was a data display still gripped in one of the corpse's hands.

Remy left Dreyla and Tosh preoccupied with the three bodies and moved through the cargo hold, up to the small bridge. Near the front console, he discovered two more bodies. One of these guys had managed to draw his pistol, which looked remarkably similar to the plasma guns Remy was used to seeing—and often using.

OK, not so unarmed after all.

He hauled one body and then the other down into the cargo hold as Dreyla and Tosh watched in eerie silence.

"Uh, what are you doing?" Dreyla asked.

He panted. "Isn't it obvious?"

Damn, these bodies are like sacks of rocks.

He let the second corpse fall. It slumped awkwardly across the first, as if the two unfortunates had perished during a bout of wrestling. He turned to Dreyla. She was clutching her stomach. Tosh's chin quivered.

"Look, the *Jay* is dead in the water. We'll fix her, but in the meantime, we have to jack this ship and get the hell outta here," he said, eyeing them both sternly. He couldn't afford for either of them to go into full-on panic mode.

They continued to stare at him.

"Listen, I know you're both freaked the hell out... but we're on a strange planet with dangerous humanoids... and we're in a ship where five people were gunned down. The gunmen are nowhere to be found."

Their expressions didn't change.

"If someone else comes nosing around for what the ship was hauling..." Remy waited to see if they would catch on.

"Oh, man, they're gonna think *we* did this." Tosh tugged off his helmet, kneaded his forehead, and glanced around at the carnage.

Remy nodded grimly, then turned to Dreyla. "So, I need you to find the ship's power generators. Because if I can't get the engines started from the bridge, you may have to fire them up manually."

"Captain?" Dreyla came to life again, shaking her head rapidly. "I have no idea what kind of ship this is."

"Improvise. It can't be that different."

"Who says it can't?" She peered up at him through a scowl. It was the fear talking. Though often stubborn, she was rarely this snippy and argumentative.

"Look." Remy pointed at the data display in the dead man's hand.

"Well, what do you know," Tosh mused.

Apparently, he hadn't noticed the tablet through the carnage.

"Care to clue me in?" Dreyla asked.

"Whoa! It's in English." Tosh knelt beside the body to look closer at the screen. "Granted, there are some words I don't recognize, but still..."

"How can that be?" Dreyla asked in a small voice. "We don't even know where we are..."

"Flee now, philosophize later," Remy said. He gave her a bracing smile.

She finally nodded and stepped gingerly around the bodies toward the rear of the ship.

"Tosh, why don't you go with her," Remy asked, although it wasn't a mere request.

Tosh nodded, stood up, and then did a slow-motion pirouette before his feet slipped out from under him and he landed splat in the middle of the largest pool of blood. Slick drops of the dark-red stuff rained down everywhere, splashing across Remy's gloved hands.

"That's disgusting," Dreyla rasped out from the doorway.

Remy followed her stricken gaze. He would've laughed if he'd had time for it. Tosh was drenched in blood. Droplets fell from his nose, eyebrows, and whiskers. A thick sludge ran down his chest, which only spread out more as he got to his feet. He looked like a mad scientist performing a heart transplant without any medical training—and rather enjoying himself.

"That'll stain," Tosh said mildly, brushing off his blood-splattered gloves on his enviro suit, then followed Dreyla to the engine room.

Remy tried to dispel the ghoulish image from his mind as he headed back to the bridge. He sat down in what was obviously the pilot's chair and rifled through the control and diagnostic screens as well as the various mystery buttons on the console. Just as he was about to switch on what he hoped were the main engines, he heard a light thud behind him.

"Drey?" he asked.

But before he could turn, something hard and heavy hit the back of his head, and his world went black. Again.

Chapter 31

REMY

Voices. Angry voices. Too loud...

Remy winced and lifted one eyelid, just a crack. Any more than that, experience told him, was going to hurt. A lot.

He lay on his side atop a hard mattress. His whole head pounded. Pain radiated from a white-hot line at the base of his skull—where someone had presumably bludgeoned him. Every heartbeat brought a fresh shard of memory and another red flash behind his eyelids. He craved the cool blackness of oblivion, but his fuzzy brain wouldn't let him rest.

Dreyla!

He wrenched his second eye open. The opposite wall was close. Not enough to touch, but almost. He seemed to be in a confined but well-lit space. He shifted onto his back, spotted some weird graffiti scrolled onto the frame above him, and realized he lay on the bottom of a bunk bed. Turning to the side, he noted only one other "furnishing" in the cell, an old-fashioned toilet made of a dull metal. His enviro suit and weapons were nowhere in sight.

Bars separated him from two other cells, whose occupants he couldn't see, and a barred window faced what he figured was outside.

Drey wasn't here. Or if she was, she wasn't conscious. Otherwise, she'd be calling his name. He could only hope she was alive—and with Tosh—in some other cell nearby. Or could they possibly have escaped and returned to the *Jay*?

He'd grown tired of waking up from forced darkness. Every bone and muscle in his body begged to fall back to sleep, but he fought it. He groaned, compelling himself to sit upright on the bunk.

OK, someone sounded really pissed off. An androgynous voice. A shrill, high timbre, imperious and bitter, with a strange inflection. Not quite human. But not artificial. Accompanied by a deep, male voice, also enraged.

"They brutally murdered the entire crew," the androgynous voice screeched, "and you have not even bothered to revive him yet?"

The deeper voice didn't answer him... or her. Remy waited.

"Where is the shipment?!" came the shrill voice again.

Even in his sluggish state, Remy understood the implications. These voices were talking—or, rather, arguing—about him. He was being blamed for the killings. No, *they* were. Which meant they'd captured Drey and Tosh as well.

Damn.

Pivoting side to side, he could just make out the figure in each adjoining cell. Neither was part of his crew.

He stood up and staggered over to the barred doorway that faced the corridor. The argument, which continued to be heated, came from a nearby room.

"Hey, psst," a rough voice said from the cell to his left.

Remy turned and spotted a large, muscular man, with a bald head and deep-set eyes, unambiguously human.

The man grinned cockily. He was chewing a stick, like a reformed smoker, and he had perfected the sort of dangerous glint in his eyes that Remy had seen his fellow pirates employ when trying to intimidate people.

"Sounds like they got you for jacking the nano-biotics... and, from what I've heard, killing off the entire med crew."

Remy held the guy's badass gaze and let a silence draw out. Two could play the intimidation game.

Finally, he answered, "We didn't kill anybody; they were all dead when we got there."

The meaty guy nodded and then squinted, as if sizing him up.

Remy turned away, straining to hear the ongoing argument about him and his crew. Through the front of his cell, he spied a door leading to the room where the voices were coming from. Thick glass composed the top half of the door, allowing him to see inside.

If life back on Earth hadn't gotten so strange when the Newton's Gate incident happened—and portals hadn't started hauling creatures from across the galaxy, across time, and even from different universes—Remy probably would've been shocked at the sight of the two figures pacing in the other room.

But as it stood, he felt only mild curiosity. One of the incensed beings reminded him of an elf: lean and pale with distinctively pointy features, especially the ears. The other resembled a dwarf: short, stout, with a ruddy complexion and a long beard that always seemed to be the trademark of that species, even in fiction.

"Where am I?" Remy murmured.

"In jail, dumbass," a man said from the cell on the right.

Remy swung around and glared at him. The creep didn't seem qualified to call anyone else a dumbass.

Turning back, he noticed the badass guy on the other side rolling his eyes. Either meant as a gesture of attempted camaraderie or indicating how much the thug despised his other cellmate.

"You're in Naillik," Badass said with a grim kind of emphasis that suggested it was the worst jail, or compound, or city, a man could find himself in. The name certainly suited such a place.

"Yeah, well, what planet?" Remy asked.

Badass arched an eyebrow. "Vox."

Upon waking up in the crash-landed *Jay*, it hadn't taken long for Remy and his crew to figure out they weren't on Earth. Again, the whole giant moon and two-toned sky had confirmed as much... not to mention the bizarre beast that had nearly taken off the doc's head. The fact that people here seemed to speak English, however, was unexpected.

Remy rubbed the back of his neck. Learning that he'd washed up on a planet he'd never even remotely heard of didn't improve his throbbing headache. It only raised questions that his hazy brain didn't want to contemplate.

Besides whiskey, Remy usually avoided all psychotropic drugs, but right now, he could really use one of Tosh's weird and wonderful concoctions—the ones the doc often served him when he was injured or "under the weather."

"Funny, you don't strike me as the type who'd join those froufrou monks in Trame," Badass continued.

Remy blinked at him. Of the many things he'd been accused of during his travels, this had to top them all.

"What type do I strike you as?" he asked gruffly.

The man ignored the question and jabbed his thumb toward the window. "Alright, so you're not with them."

Remy stepped closer to the window to see what group he'd been eliminated from. The view, surprisingly, encompassed a busy thoroughfare. Though humans seemed to predominate in the crowds milling around outside, he also spotted a smattering of elves and dwarves, along with several robots. His silly hope that he might spy his crew out there, shuffling around in disguise, was utterly dashed. Nobody even cast a glance at the jail cell.

Then his gaze landed on the giant billboard screen looming across the street. It featured several purple-robed individuals—the so-called froufrou monks—posing in front of a monastic temple. Beneath the image, he could discern a series of dates in thick black lettering, plus the typical "join us" pitch. The call to spirituality and salvation from eternal damnation was indeed universal.

"Look, I'm from off-planet," Remy explained. "Our froufrou monks wear orange."

He glanced at the sign again.

"And tend to be skinny old men, not hot young women."

The man snorted. "Everybody on Vox is from off-planet."

Remy regarded the man properly this time, searching beyond the badass exterior, noting his merciless eyes, his sinister grin. The dude had to be a pirate or at least a member of organized crime. Remy had faced men like him almost his entire life.

Or maybe it just takes one to know one?

The man stepped toward his cell and shoved his hand through the adjoining bars. "I'm Yercer Taul."

Even the name screamed, *I'm a criminal!*

Without hesitation, Remy accepted the man's hand and shook it with a business-like smile. "Remy Bechet."

Yercer Taul's grip was tight but Remy reciprocated, keeping his smile in place and resisting the man's attempts to twist his hand into a submissive position.

What an idiot.

"Hey, Yercer!" a woman's voice barked. "Sit the hell down!"

Chapter 32

LILLY

Lilly ramped up her glare at the beefy pain in her ass, ensuring he got the hint.

Yercer smirked back, released the newest prisoner's hand, and sank onto his bunk. He swung one leg over the other and rolled up his convict-tunic sleeves to reveal thick, hairy forearms, making a big show of getting comfortable. His gaze yo-yoed between her and the new guy, as if he expected some form of entertainment to ensue.

But the program was on a commercial break. The man of the hour, who'd apparently just awakened from his inconvenient coma, hadn't budged from where he'd stood to shake hands with Yercer. As the seconds ticked by, he remained perfectly still. Only his gleaming, hazel eyes moved as they tracked her and her two companions hovering in front of the cells.

Like a bird of prey.

Lilly's husband had had a fondness for birds of prey. He'd especially adored talconians and could watch videos of them for hours. Part of his fascination had arisen from how the raptors stood still, deathly still, before they pounced. He'd even tried to have one bioengineered on Vox, but it hadn't worked out.

She shook away the memory and cocked her head at Milo, the dworg rep from Yerdua, and Jacer, the aflin from Elocin, indicating they should come closer to the cell. "He won't bite."

Milo stepped forward with hunched shoulders. "You sure? He looks just the type."

"Cybernetics scan was clean," she said, checking the notes on her tablet.

Just a regular human, if a well-toned one. No implants or fancy stuff. Nothing that could gnash through bars of titanium alloy.

After a pause, Jacer shuffled closer as well, frowning at the new prisoner.

Lilly was thankful for their silence. Milo and Jacer had

just spent the last thirty minutes blaming her for something she had zero control over. If she had to listen to another syllable of Jacer's high-pitched, querulous voice or one more of Milo's forlorn sighs, she might just have to kill herself. Or them.

At least she seemed to have convinced the prickly duo that someone had moved up the med shipment without consulting any of them, including her, and that by the time she and her team had arrived at the unusual drop location, the crew was dead and the nano-biotics were gone. But it had been a struggle to persuade them—and everyone else with a vested interest.

Of course, what had actually happened on the med ship was still a total mystery, and as a rule, she didn't like mysteries.

Her eyes panned to the dark-haired prisoner, absorbing him thoroughly for the first time. Until now, after all, he hadn't been conscious enough to truly assess.

Lilly held his insolent gaze which, surprisingly for a convict—or, well, a male—didn't wander across her curves, mentally stripping her. Just for that, she'd let him eat a decent meal tonight. If he provided answers.

Before she could start questioning him, though, the prisoner spoke first.

"Where's my crew?" he demanded, his tone reasonable but with an undercurrent of steel.

These naturally authoritative types pissed her off. What

business did criminal scum have to sound capable and rational?

She took a step closer to the bars. "The madman is sedated in the psych wing at the med center."

A hint of a smile tugged at one corner of the prisoner's mouth. But his eyes were still fixed on her, unblinking, serious.

"The girl..." she said, suddenly sensing how important this was to him, "is at the juvenile detention center. We're still trying to determine if she's responsible for being at the crime scene, or if you kidnapped and coerced her into aiding you."

For what it was worth, she'd decided to give the cooperative approach a shot first—exchanging what she knew in the hope he'd do the same.

The prisoner's shoulder and arm muscles bunched up. He shifted his weight, glanced down at his feet and then back to her face. "First off," he said in a quietly cold voice, "I didn't kidnap Dreyla. She's part of my crew, practically my daughter."

"Practically?" Milo sneered. "Oh, is that what you call it?"

Lilly shot Milo a warning glance. Heckling wouldn't help the situation.

The prisoner, however, didn't noticeably react.

"Well, Captain... Remy Bechet," she said, consulting her notes, "you have a strange way of raising a daughter."

Not that she had any relevant experience, but she was pretty sure the average sixteen-year-old shouldn't be stealing meds and aiding her *practically*-father in killing off a team of innocent medics, along with all the other atrocities they'd doubtlessly committed prior to arriving in Naillik.

Milo brushed past her, grasped the bars, and stared Bechet down. "Come on, where's the shipment of nano-biotics, you no-good piece of scum?"

"You got it all wrong, dwarf. We didn't steal anything, and we didn't kill anybody."

Bechet's steady, deadly tone rang of the truth. Which was a pity. Because this situation had just gotten a whole lot more complicated.

Lilly turned to Milo, expecting him to take offense. The dworg remained silent and unreactive.

Jacer pushed past him. "*That* is a likely story."

Bechet lifted his gaze to the aflin. "We found the ship like that... everyone was already dead."

Scoffing, Jacer pivoted toward Lilly. "He is in league with Taul and Darkbur and all the other Bane scum!" For emphasis, he flapped his spindly fingers toward the caged man.

"Easy there, elf, I just met this guy." Bechet pointed his thumb over his shoulder, aiming it squarely at Yercer, who was gobbling up every word of this heated exchange.

Jacer bristled.

Lilly exhaled slowly. "Jacer, Milo, we just saw them meet." She indicated Yercer still sitting on his bunk. "So, he's at least telling the truth about that."

"No, darlin'," Yercer said, smiling broadly, his hands clasped behind his head. "We're all in it together. He's one of us."

Bechet swung around. "Piss off, fat man."

Yercer's face morphed from amusement to anger in a flash. He leapt off his bunk and slammed his body against the bars, trying to grasp Bechet. But his stocky upper arms were too thick to reach him.

Bechet didn't even blink. He grabbed one of Yercer's hands, twisted and bent it at the same time, and ultimately forced the much larger man to his knees.

Lilly had instinctively reached for her weapon, but the confrontation had happened so fast, she'd only managed to cup her hand around the grip of her pistol. She'd had no time to unholster it before Yercer was on the floor.

After a reflective moment, though, she decided against drawing her weapon. She'd let this one play out.

"Come on, pudge, tell the truth," Bechet growled.

But Yercer wasn't that easy. He grabbed ahold of Bechet's other arm and wrenched it through the bars, into his cell. It was fair play, but a secret part of Lilly wanted to see Captain Bechet break Yercer's wrist.

Which was exactly what he did. With a snap that made her wince, the thug's wrist bent into a grotesque, unnatural position. Any other human would have released his grip, but, with a stifled yelp, Yercer yanked down further on Bechet's arm.

The captain released his adversary's broken wrist and pulled with all his might on the man's other arm, which brought Yercer's body back up against the bars. He then sent a fist through the bars, punching Yercer's massive head. If he'd aimed for the big man's left eye, then he'd hit his target.

Finally, Yercer released Bechet's arm and stumbled back to his bunk, squinting one eye, cradling his wrist, and growling death threats.

Bechet, meanwhile, calmly stepped away from the bars. The whole fight had taken less than ten seconds, and in that time, he'd dealt with one of the biggest, meanest criminals on the planet with apparent ease. That made him either extremely capable or extremely lucky. Extremely dangerous, too.

Of course, it also demonstrated a certain foolhardiness. Not wise to make an enemy of one of Darkbur's top guys.

"Where are you from, Remy Bechet?" Lilly asked, keeping her voice as cool as possible as she surveyed the damage and the alarmed reactions of her companions.

"First, how do you know my name? Second, how is it that you're speaking English?"

"The girl, Dreyla, she told me your name..." She looked up and met his steadfast gaze. "And I have no idea what English is. We just call it the common tongue."

A flash of something vulnerable in his eyes softened him, just for a moment, before his expression hardened again.

"I'm from off-planet," he said gruffly. "Really far off-planet."

Chapter 33

DREYLA

Dreyla sat huddled on a chair near a barred window, trying to ignore the echoing voices around her—mainly so she could concentrate on hatching an escape plan. She'd already spent three days in this craphole "juvenile detention center"—and she was beyond sick of its scratchy clothing, cardboard food, and dreary decor.

She also longed for some rest. Without Tosh's handy adrenaline blockers, she'd found it tough to sleep in this unsettling place. Not only because of her lumpy bunk and mistrust of strangers, but also due to her anxiety over Remy and Tosh—and what might be happening to them.

It had taken her all of fifteen minutes to figure out that the JDC was essentially a drug-rehab joint for female children and teenagers. Most of the inmates were too spaced out or too miserable to even consider fleeing.

Despite keeping to herself as she tended to do, she'd overheard whispers from the other kids about scoring scat—the drug of choice in this crazy little town, just outside of which she, Remy, and Tosh had inconveniently crash-landed. Apparently, the girls here lived, breathed, and dreamt of scat. Their conversations were very limited.

"Didn't you hear me? I asked if you had any."

Dreyla looked up. A tall, stocky girl about her age—noticeable for her woefully self-dyed, blue-and-purple hair—loomed over her. Dreyla assumed she was the detainee "in charge." She thought she'd heard one of the other kids call her Mosi.

"I told you yesterday," Dreyla said, feigning boredom, "I don't have anything for you."

The girl poked her face into Dreyla's personal space, almost nose to nose. "Don't talk down to me, little girl." She then jabbed her, hard, with two fingers to the chest.

Dreyla had seen this confrontation coming. About five minutes after discovering that most of the kids here were either hooked on scat or recovering from it, she'd figured out the behemoth poking her was gonna be trouble.

She rose slowly. "Don't do that."

"Oh, I'll do whatever I want," Mosi shot back, glaring through narrowed eyes.

She poked Dreyla again. Same place, just harder.

In a flash, Dreyla grabbed Mosi's wrist, twisted and bent it, and forced the girl—incidentally almost twice her size—to fall to her knees. Remy had taught his daughter that move a long time ago. Nearly guaranteed to incapacitate an enemy, even without breaking any bones.

Mosi unleashed a shriek of pain. "You bitch!"

"That's enough!" Beadic, the woman in charge of the detention center, waddled over. She was even larger than Mosi, but unlike the strong, stocky girl, Beadic was simply fat.

Dreyla released her grip and stepped back. Beadic wrapped her fingers around the back of Dreyla's neck, pinching the flesh with her sharp nails, just enough to sting, and led her out of the room.

She had already learned the hard way not to struggle when Beadic did this. The first time she'd tried to pull away, the woman had dug her talons in, leaving vicious gashes behind.

So, Drey allowed Beadic to drag her down the hallway and into a private office, where the obese woman shoved her newest charge onto a rosy velvet couch along one wall. Then Beadic shut the door and plunked herself down next to Drey, regarding the girl in silence.

Dreyla cringed. The woman was clearly unstable. Brutal and angry one moment and then—she waited for it, her gut clenching in disgust—Beadic's fingers slid from her neck, slowly trailing down her shoulder. She shivered. This ogre was attempting to flirt with her again.

Maybe schizophrenia and bipolar disorder were common in the universe she, Remy, and Tosh had ended up in. Maybe the people here all swung between extremes. But, more than likely, Beadic was just a sick, perverted bitch who took advantage of her position in order to grope and seduce the young girls forced to reside here.

Great way to rehab.

The first day Beadic had come on to her, Dreyla had played the inexperienced card and simply ignored the woman. The second day, when Beadic had tried the same thing again, she'd made the mistake of being too forceful in rebuffing the woman's unsavory advances. That time, Drey had witnessed Beadic's anger flare up, only to be saved when one of the staff members had stumbled into the office to inform her boss of a brawl.

This time, there would be no interruption. And that was by careful design.

Dreyla's blood went cold. She had to choose between being compliant or getting hurt, and frankly, she didn't have any experience with sex—consensual or otherwise. True, Drey would often tease Remy by pretending she'd had oodles of secret encounters, but in reality, she hadn't. How *could* she, when her only companions were her dad, a grandfatherly doctor, and a bunch of middle-aged pirates, all of whom knew they'd be dead if they so much as glanced at her wrong?

Her skin prickled. She couldn't deal with this, whatever *this* was going to be. Her thin tunic made her feel horribly exposed.

No, that's it, I'd rather die.

Dreyla reached toward the woman. The greedy smile stretching Beadic's plump, pink lips showed that she thought Drey would play ball.

"There we go," she cooed softly. "Better to be nice, isn't it?"

Instead, Dreyla grabbed the collar of the woman's shirt and pulled down with all her strength, stretching the fabric, ripping a hole in it, and revealing Beadic's bra.

The move had temporarily bound the woman's arms in her own shirt. Recognizing her advantage, Dreyla grabbed a lamp from the table next to the couch and brought it crashing down onto the side of the woman's head.

Beadic groaned and slumped toward the carpet. She rolled off the couch and came to rest in front of the desk.

Dreyla stepped around her and opened the office door to see if anyone had heard.

Six other girls, gathered outside the door, tumbled into

the room. One of them screeched when she saw Beadic lying unconscious on the office floor. Luckily, another girl clamped her hand over the squealer's mouth.

Dreyla needed to make this quick.

She turned back to the office. Fifty small lockers lined one wall. She glanced down at the bracelet she'd been forced to wear upon arrival. It bore the number 1130. She searched for that locker. It was one of the lowest ones.

She tried the knob, but the units were all secured. Normally, she could pick a lock in less than fifteen seconds, given the proper tools, but these required an official thumbprint. She regarded the large woman on the floor.

This wouldn't be easy, but Drey had no other option.

She turned back to the girls, who were all watching her in complete fascination.

Mosi pushed through the group for a closer look. "Holy crap. You knocked that evil bitch out?"

Dreyla eyed her for a moment and then threw caution to the wind. "Mosi, if you wanna get outta this cesspool, come and help me move her."

Mosi, either despite or because of their previous encounter, didn't hesitate. She entered the office quickly and, regardless of her injured wrist, grasped Beadic's legs. Together, the two girls dragged the rotund woman over to the lockers. Mosi held Beadic's hand up to Dreyla's locker, which promptly buzzed, followed by the telltale click of a door opening.

Before Dreyla could retrieve its contents, though, Mosi had pulled the woman's thumb up to the next locker and repeated the process. Dreyla abandoned her own locker and helped her cohort instead. They worked together, sweating and cursing Beadic's deadweight, until they'd sprung open all the lockers. Meanwhile, the other girls milled around the office, hysterically grasping their long-lost possessions.

Drey heard muted squeals of delight and moans of recognition. Some lamentations that someone had taken their drugs.

Most of them only had a few scraps of apparel, maybe some mementos if they were lucky. Dreyla was pleased to discover all her clothes and accessories were still here—even her knives. The sheriff had confiscated her guns and the enviro suit but had allowed Beadic to deal with the rest of her stuff.

Dreyla dressed quickly, sheathing her knives in the holsters strapped to her hips and thighs. Then she bundled the scratchy, gray inmate's tunic in a ball and flung it into a garbage-disposal unit.

Wow, that feels so much better.

"How're we getting out, though?"

Dreyla turned to Mosi, who was squeezing herself into some bizarre strappy dress crafted from an iridescent leather that complemented her blue-and-purple hair and made her

221

look even more badass. The outfit also accentuated her blue eyes, which radiated an intelligence not apparent before.

"Guard that door," Drey told her. "We're going out the front."

Because now it was *we*. Funny how a taste of freedom could bring people together. All the other inmates had fled, no doubt fearing they'd get caught red-handed.

Dreyla moved around Beadic's desk to access her system display. Gritting her teeth, she pressed the most obvious button and prayed that it would be similar to what she was used to. The display flashed to life. She scrolled through some menus and found the building-security section. Unfortunately, it required a password.

"Well, damn," she muttered.

She retraced her steps and managed to pull up a source-code screen. It had the same vulnerability as many of the systems she'd accessed over the years—for the countless hack jobs she'd pulled for Remy. Scanning through the various functions, she found the backdoor she sought. She typed feverishly, and a moment later, the building-security section appeared, in bright and flashy 3D on the screen.

"Cool..." Mosi said, craning her neck to see from the doorway. "That what I think it is?"

Dreyla nodded. She found the system locks and released them. *Ping. Ping. Ping.*

Just outside Beadic's office lay the inner doors separating the reception area from the rest of the facility. The familiar *whoosh* of them sliding open made Mosi's eyes grow even wider.

"Let's get outta here," Dreyla said.

Chapter 34

REMY

Remy sat in an uncomfortable chair, his hands locked to the table in hard, steel cuffs he had no chance of breaking free from. He had found himself in more than one interrogation room over the years, but this particular situation was utterly screwy. The sheriff, the dworg, and the aflin were all here. After having used the e-word again, he had been corrected by the last man to enter the room—namely, Mayor Jett Cansen, a man on the verge of cardiac arrest if ever there was one.

He had quickly learned that all three races spoke a common tongue, which was, as far as he was concerned, English, no matter what they chose to call it. Apparently, the dworgs and aflins each had their own language, which they spoke among themselves.

But now his lessons were over, and his captors were the ones posing the questions.

"I'll ask you again. Where are the drugs?" Sheriff Lilly Greyson leaned closer, and he noticed the delicate rings of lilac circling her brown irises.

No two ways about it, this woman was damn attractive, even if his current predicament shouldn't be putting such notions into his dumb skull.

She sighed impatiently. "If we don't distribute them to those that need it, an awful lot of people are gonna die."

It was as bad as he'd suspected. Barely conscious and he was already public enemy number one. All he could do was repeat the same mantra.

"Sheriff, like I told you, we crashed our ship not far from that area. We just stumbled onto the scene. Right before you showed up, I guess." He sighed. "And as I already said, we spotted six armed men fleeing the scene. No doubt they're the homicidal thieves you're looking for."

Unlike most women, this one was unreadable. He didn't know whether to appeal to her vanity, her greed, her compassion, or something else entirely.

"He is lying." Jacer, the elf—or, rather, *aflin*—jiggled on the spot. "He and his people were trying to steal the ship!"

"Why would he hide the drugs and then return to steal the ship?" Milo, the dworg, challenged.

"To hide the evidence," Mayor Cansen said, flashing a knowing grin at Remy.

The sheriff seemed to consider that a distinct possibility, her eyebrows drawing together pensively.

"But that's crazy," Remy said. "Look, go find my ship. That'll prove—"

"We've sent people to locate this ship of yours," she snapped. "We'll see if it checks out. But that still won't prove you didn't kill the med crew and swipe the shipment."

Feeling both defeated and irritated, Remy sank against the hard, unyielding chair. Just then, the door opened and another large man, slightly smaller than Yercer and some twenty years older, stalked in.

"So, you caught the murdering scum," he said by way of greeting.

"Who is this idiot?" Remy snarled.

Probably not the smartest thing to do.

The man's fist collided with Remy's cheekbone. The old man moved way faster than he should for someone his age. And man, did he pack a punch.

The sheriff rose. "Back off, Gono, this is my station. And my case."

The man slowly stepped back and gazed down in amusement as Remy hunched up his shoulder and tried to wipe the blood from his nose. Not really fair to mess up the face of a man whose hands were locked to a table.

"Gono Darkbur is my name, and you are?" the brute asked.

"This, Gono, is Captain Remy Bechet," the sheriff said, "and he was just about to tell us—"

"—that we didn't kill those people," Remy repeated. "We didn't steal your meds. And I'm not from around here."

The blood trickling down his face and into his collar aggravated him, but the sheriff didn't seem to have any sympathy for his plight.

"He's lying," a familiar voice said from the hallway.

Remy's jaw almost hit the table as his gaze met the sharp, green eyes of the person he'd least expected to see in the flesh... Commander Tara Shaw.

"Oh, hell, no," he muttered.

While no longer wearing her UNSF uniform, she still portrayed the arrogance of her rank in her white, razor-sharp bodysuit and her furry shoulder wrap, which she might or might not have personally skinned from an unidentified dead animal. She had tried to hide a recent gash on her forehead by letting her hair down. She must've slipped through the portal and crashed on the planet just as he, Dreyla, and Tosh had.

"I've had dealings with him in Bane, you see," Shaw said with affected laziness, waving her metallic hand. Her terrible eyes gleamed when she looked at him; she clearly relished this moment.

"She's a lying bitch," Remy growled. Glancing at Gono,

he added, "You don't know what you have there."

"Sheriff Greyson," Gono said, pointedly ignoring him, "this is one of my newest associates, Tara Shaw."

The sheriff eyed the woman. The only hint of any misgiving was a slight upward tilt of an eyebrow, and even then, Remy couldn't be sure. But at least they didn't shake hands.

"Shaw here tells me he's been smuggling scat onto the planet for the last year," Gono continued in a deceptively soft voice.

"I don't even know what that is," Remy said, bracing himself for another hit.

He'd started to get the distinct impression that he wouldn't be able to talk his way out of this dilemma. From the look of things, the aflin thought he was guilty, and Gono was using Shaw to support that conclusion.

On the other hand, the dworg still seemed skeptical, so there might be some hope. But Remy still couldn't get a read on the sheriff. Her pleasing curves only confused the situation. Same with the crooked smile he'd seen her shoot one of her deputies.

Damn, he was cursed to fall for pretty faces and fleeting acts of kindness. His fuzzy brain didn't need this distraction.

Not now anyway.

Then the sheriff did something unexpected. She

rounded on Gono Darkbur. "I don't know what's going on yet, but somehow, I get the feeling you're behind all this."

Gono's face turned dark crimson, but Shaw's superior smile didn't falter.

"Yes, where were you, Darkbur?" Milo's deep voice boomed out. "How come none of your people showed up at the landing site yesterday? When the shipment was originally expected?"

"I, too, find that a little strange," Jacer said, his frail voice quivering.

"Yes," the sheriff joined in. "Given that we purposely kept the news from going out over the broad-wave, hoping to avoid widespread panic, there was no way for you to know the shipment had been hijacked and the med crew killed."

For a moment, the silence seemed incriminating.

"Well, I have my sources," Gono finally said. "Nothing happens on Vox without me knowing about it."

"Perhaps," the sheriff replied. "But I still find the whole thing awfully suspicious."

Remy liked where this interrogation was going. The focus had shifted off him and onto this Gono Darkbur character, whom Shaw was obviously working for.

While reflecting on his archnemesis, he caught a quick glance from her. He couldn't tell if she was about to draw a weapon and shoot him or if she was almost as confused as he was.

Man, she'd moved fast to find a new master—even though this guy seemed like a low-rent version of Larker Max... which was saying a lot. Obviously, she'd gotten caught in the same weird green portal that the *Jay* had. But where had she crashed and how had she already found employment on the planet? More importantly, was her ship still functioning?

"As the official representative of Bane and the surrounding territory," Gono blustered, "I take great offense to the accusation that I—or, indeed, any of my people—had anything to do with this incident."

In other words, he didn't deny it.

Shaw leaned in and whispered something to Gono.

"And I'll be filing a complaint with the Vox Council when they reconvene," he added.

The sheriff took two steps toward him and raised her chin up to look him straight in the face. Remy found himself smiling. This woman had moxie.

"You do that," the sheriff said tonelessly.

The room fell quiet again. For several seconds, everybody avoided everyone else's eyes, and then Gono turned and left the room.

Shaw lingered a moment, a tiny smile crossing her glossy lips as she gave Remy a pitying once-over. Then she followed Gono out.

When the door closed shut again, Remy looked up at the sheriff. "So, you'll be letting me go then, right?"

No verbal response. She merely gazed at him and scowled.

Despite her contemptuous expression, he still couldn't help but admire the woman's beauty. Her sculpted legs, shapely backside, and ample chest would've been mesmerizing enough, but she'd also been blessed with a lovely, heart-shaped face, silky black hair, and incredible eyes. Remy could've gotten lost in those two radiant orbs. Strong, intelligent, and vivacious—with a hint of sadness.

Normally, he wouldn't have minded the prospect of being jailed in a place run by such an enticing creature. Seeing Sheriff Lilly Greyson every day would've been a stellar way to pass the time—a far better view than those offered by all the other cells he'd occupied... and Remy had experienced quite a slew over the years.

But regardless of the temptation she posed, it wasn't enough to placate him. No, he couldn't stay—and he certainly couldn't waste any more time. He needed to liberate himself from this crazy situation, find Drey and Tosh, and get off this backwards-assed planet as soon as possible.

So, since reason had yet to free him, he decided to try charm instead.

Why not go full-tilt boogie and see where that gets me?

At some point during Remy's rambling thoughts, the sheriff had turned away from him. Now, with her arms crossed beneath her alluring breasts, she leaned against the wall and stared at the door. Perhaps lost in her own thoughts.

For a few seconds, he simply watched her.

"Sheriff," he finally said in a husky voice, "look at me." Then he arched an eyebrow and unleashed a roguish grin.

With a dramatic sigh, she turned toward him again... and stifled a chuckle.

OK, not exactly the reaction I was hoping for...

His charisma typically served him well, but not this time. Of course, to be fair, the sheriff was like no woman he'd ever encountered. She had him all tangled up inside, making him question everything.

Frowning, he decided to switch back to pleading mode. "Seriously, do I look like someone who could do such an awful thing?"

He hoped honesty and sincerity would sway the woman. True, it had rarely worked in the past. But there was a first time for everything.

Chapter 35

LILLY

Despite the prisoner's lingering question, an awkward silence ensued long after Gono's departure. Milo and Jacer had slipped out to attend mandatory virtual meetings about the missing shipment of nano-biotics, leaving Lilly and Cansen alone with the man in custody.

"Just check out my ship," Bechet insisted again, "and you'll know I'm telling the truth."

Lilly smiled mirthlessly.

The truth.

Would that be the same truth as attested by every other guilty man, woman, aflin, or dworg who had ever sat in that chair?

He was wasting his breath. She had learned to ignore the pleas, no matter how heartfelt their delivery.

She had also noted how tense he'd seemed around Tara Shaw. There was definitely something going on between those two. Clearly, nobody here was innocent, but would Lilly have time to unravel what the hell was really happening before all her Rot-infested citizens died? No, she wouldn't. Her tolerance for mind games had hit rock bottom. She just wanted those meds—justice came second.

The man on the other side of the table didn't look like a sadistic killer, but then again, looks could be deceiving. Case in point: the suave, well-dressed Gono Darkbur. And Bechet did have a slight Bane-ish air about him—the scruffy, renegade, anti-establishment, fringe-living aura of those who didn't want to deal with laws and taxes and other municipal inconveniences.

"Just out of curiosity," Bechet said, "how long was I knocked out?"

Lilly sighed. "Three days."

"Three days?!" He straightened his back, the cuffs clanking against the table. "Why didn't you wake me up sooner?"

"My thoughts exactly," Cansen grumbled.

Lilly shot the mayor an annoyed look. "I understand how critical this situation is. We need to retrieve those meds as soon as possible." She sighed again. "Unfortunately, while apprehending Captain Bechet and his cohorts... let's just say one of my deputies got a little overzealous—"

"Yeah, thanks for that," Remy said. "My head's killing me. But none of that matters now... I need to see Dreyla and Tosh. I need to know they're OK."

She avoided his direct gaze. This had become a constant refrain with him. "You know I can't let you," she said. "Not until we know more."

"You mean, after you find my ship?"

"Yes, one of my teams is checking out your story. Until then..."

Mayor Cansen cleared his throat. He seemed more than ready to convict the captain, mopping his brow and shifting his portly frame from leg to leg in frustration. Less because of any conviction of the captain's guilt and more because the story of the dead med crew had already hit the streets. Strange, since it hadn't been officially announced. Maybe that, too, was Gono's fault.

Cansen wasn't a bad man, but serving as the mayor of Naillik often made him act out of political motivations, which sometimes conflicted with what his constituents required to stay safe. Announcing that the powers-that-be had caught the murdering thieves would please the public. Spending days figuring out the actual guilty party and *then* rescuing the meds wouldn't offer the immediate results Cansen sought in the ongoing popularity contest of being an elected official.

Of course, none of that would matter if the nans remained lost. A rising mortality rate would trump all other news.

"Sheriff," the mayor harrumphed, "I think we can see that this man is, in the very least, the sort of scum that would do something like that."

"Hey, jerkwad, who are you calling scum?" Bechet asked.

Cansen's face reddened even more than usual. "And who are you calling jerkwad?"

Lilly squeezed her eyes shut. OK, this wasn't helping. Like that of her newest prisoner, her head was pounding—not from an uncharacteristic bludgeoning from Deputy Davis, but due to the extreme stress she'd been under for the past three days.

Everyone—from Mayor Cansen to the faraway Vox Council—had repeatedly demanded that she rouse their primary suspect from his trauma-induced coma. Beyond having a medic treat him for a possible concussion, however, she'd staunchly refused to wake him prematurely.

Yes, someone needed to answer for such heinous murders. Yes, she desperately needed to reclaim the meds. And yes, having the same argument for three days straight had tested her resolve.

But from the start, something hadn't added up about this entire situation. Who'd approved the altered date and location for the shipment? How had this joker and his two unlikely companions gotten the drop on five armed medics? And where the hell had they dragged the crates of nano-biotics? To a ship full of their accomplices? Then why'd they stick around to be caught with five corpses?

She found it particularly strange that she'd never seen or heard of the odd trio before. True, she didn't know every criminal on the planet, but unlawful types usually appeared on her radar long before committing such unspeakable crimes.

Still, she couldn't have this man—whoever the hell he was—verbally sparring with Naillik's mayor. But before she could reprimand the prisoner, he started talking again.

"You think I *wanted* to land—*crash*—on your stupid planet? Trust me, if that portal hadn't sprung out of nowhere, we'd be safely on the other side of the moon right now."

Interesting.

Vox's moon wasn't exactly difficult to reach, so either this guy was crazy, lying creatively, or telling the truth.

She'd seen a report from the Vox Council about some mysterious, often-fleeting portals opening close to the home planets, but nothing like that had ever happened near Vox. At least as far as she knew.

Lilly exchanged a glance with Cansen, whose curt shake of the head indicated he thought Bechet had ascended to another level of crapola. And it kind of sounded like it.

She strolled to the window to buy a little time. It was on such occasions she wished she had the same hard heart Tim had possessed when it came to dealing with suspects. He'd always been able to mentally torment them when necessary. Likewise, all she'd have to do was threaten to harm Bechet's friends, the girl and the old man, to elicit some answers. That would surely work, as the so-called captain seemed to care for them, especially the girl.

But she wasn't Tim. Not yet.

"So... you're telling us you're from an entirely different, what, galaxy?" she asked, unable to keep her pitch from rising into the octave of incredulity.

"Or universe," Bechet said, scowling now.

"Oh, come on," Cansen snapped.

Bechet twisted his head to address the mayor head-on. "When a bunch of scientists—asshats much like yourself—tried to build a gateway to travel faster throughout our galaxy—"

"This was on your home world?" she asked, cutting in over Cansen's protests.

Bechet nodded. "Out in space, anyway... and they mucked it up. Damn thing exploded, and the end result..." He sighed. "Well, now we have to deal with the freaking random-ness of portals, leading us God-knows-where."

"And you expect us to believe that these *portals* can in-stantly transport you from planet to planet?" Cansen asked, punctuating the question with a loud snort.

He looked ready to punch the restrained captain. And Lilly was tempted to let him do it.

Bechet, as if sensing this, spoke rapidly, focusing on her. "Well, the idea was to utilize Newton's Gate to travel aboard a spaceship to anywhere in the galaxy, or perhaps even in the universe... but when it exploded, it ended up... how did they explain it? Look, I'm no physicist, but it created a, um, tear in space-time, which resulted in an infinite number of portals popping up on the planet and out in space."

"And why did you fly your ship—"

"He doesn't have a ship," Cansen butted in.

"—through the portal to Vox?" Lilly finished.

Her tablet flashed. Apparently, Deputy Davis wanted to chat.

Wow, what bad timing.

She reverted her gaze back to Bechet. He was taking deep breaths, as if striving to calm himself down. Something told her he was used to being the one calling the shots.

"The portal I was trying to go through would've led back

to our moon," Bechet explained. "The one near my home world. But another appeared in its place, and we accidentally flew the *Jay* to your planet instead. That portal must've led to just outside your atmo." He shrugged awkwardly. "Can't say for sure. Cuz my crewmates and I passed out on the way down."

Lilly's tablet flashed again. She pressed her lips together. "Mayor," she said in a tight voice, "if you would follow me, please?"

She rose and Cansen trailed her.

On a whim, she looked back at the prisoner. "I think we have a report coming in from my team." Then she opened the door.

Davis stood in the hallway, ready to pounce.

"What is it?" she asked.

He cleared his throat. "They didn't find anything."

Cansen snapped his fingers. "See? He did it."

"I don't know," Lilly said.

She was examining the video feed from the mission. A typical Vox desert scene.

"What's that?" She pointed at a large swath of sand that seemed displaced in an odd way—by something much, much bigger than a man.

"Yeah, could've been a ship there," Davis said. "Brand noticed that, too," he added with a note of pride.

The mayor snorted in disgust. "Just means he had accomplices."

"Maybe," Lilly hedged. "But the tracks from the crates led elsewhere."

With a resigned sigh, she slipped back into the interrogation room. She locked eyes with Bechet, whose crestfallen face indicated he'd heard about the missing ship.

Milo and Jacer squeezed past Davis as they reentered the room. Their emergency meetings had apparently ended, and neither looked happy.

"Sheriff, if we can't figure this out, things are going to get bad," Milo said.

Lilly looked at him sharply. "For whom?" She already knew things were bad, but the way he spoke made it sound even worse.

"For all of us," he added.

"But especially for you here in Naillik," Jacer cut in. "Our council in Elocin is—"

"Blaming us?" She shook her head. "Come on, Jacer, that's complete crap, you know it is!"

"Since the plan most likely originated in Bane," Jacer said in a reedy, toneless voice, "and that is still considered a human establishment—"

"But there are almost as many aflins and dworgs there," Lilly countered.

"I'm afraid Yerdua feels the same way." Milo, at least, sounded genuinely sympathetic.

Brand dashed toward the open door, almost knocking

Davis over in her excitement. He clasped her shoulders to steady her.

"Sheriff!" she panted. "The girls escaped!"

"Girls?" Lilly stared at her red-cheeked deputy, nonplussed.

"From the JDC! The drug addicts!"

"Who escaped?" Lilly asked, already suspecting.

"All of them. But it was instigated by that new girl, Dreyla."

Son of a bitch.

She turned toward Bechet, whose self-satisfied grin made her want to pummel his annoyingly attractive face. Maybe the time had come to torture some answers out of him after all.

Given her luck, though, the infuriating pirate would likely enjoy it.

THE END (FOR NOW)

The adventure continues in ***The Thrill Is Gone***, the second book in the ***Galactic Blues*** series.

Follow Us

We hope you've enjoyed **Cross Road Blues**, the first book in the **Galactic Blues** series. The adventure continues in **The Thrill Is Gone**, the second book in the **Galactic Blues** series.

Join the D.L. Martone Newsletter
(https://dlmartone.com/follow-d-l-martone)

We know you love your freedom, so we promise not to bombard you with junk mail. We'll only notify you on occasion about new releases, giveaways, and recommendations.

Of course, if you did enjoy **Cross Road Blues**, please consider leaving a positive review on Amazon. Thanks in advance! LEAVE REVIEW HERE

(https://www.amazon.com/dp/B08SHSHLVB)

About the Authors

D.L. Martone is the joint pen name of husband-wife duo Daniel and Laura Martone. Part-time residents of New Orleans and northern Michigan, the Martones travel the country in their mobile writing studio, a cozy RV dubbed *Serenity*. As you might have guessed, they're huge fans of *Firefly*, which is why they remodeled the interior of their travel trailer to resemble Captain Reynolds' beloved spaceship. Together, they enjoy writing urban fantasy, post-apoc zombie fiction, fantasy LitRPG/GameLit, cozy mysteries, and, of course, space opera.

Acknowledgments

As always, we appreciate the support from our friends, families, and fellow writers—as well as the inspiration gleaned from the amazing characters and riveting plots of *Firefly*, *Defiance*, *Dark Matter*, *The Expanse*, and *The Mandalorian*. We're so thankful such awesome sci-fi shows exist.

Of course, we couldn't have started this series—or finished this book—without the love and support of each other and our beloved kitty, Ruby Azazel.

Lastly, we're grateful to you, our fellow space-opera fans, for joining Remy and his crew on their misadventures across the multiverse.